Praise for

WHERE I AM

"The poignant account of a translator struggling to translate herself into a multitude of uncomfortable roles in a language and culture not her own. *Where I Am* serves up heaping portions of yearning, passion, alienation, and regret, and establishes Dana Shem-Ur as one of the rising stars of the new Israeli literature."

—JOSHUA COHEN,
Pulitzer Prize-winning author of *The Netanyahus*

"A formidable, stirring, and beautifully written novel, spectacular in its ability to penetrate the souls of its characters, juggling love, power dynamics, and staggeringly human ambitions while offering an ironic examination of the social and cultural codes of our time."

—NIR BARAM,
author of *World Shadow* and *Good People*

"In unfailingly elegant prose, *Where I Am* makes us peek at the consciousness of a foreigner who is herself trying to peek at the consciousnesses of French natives she treats with derision and anguish. It's a funny and poignant novel, strikingly resonant with the condition of foreignness plaguing so many around the world."

—EVA ILLOUZ,
author of *Why Love Hurts* and *The End of Love*

"An impressive and mature debut about a woman's search for identity and for her place in life. Or rather, her places in life: in society, in her career, in her relationship, her motherhood, her body and her sexuality, as well as her actual geographical location. A pleasurable read."

—ASSAF GAVRON,
author of *The Hilltop*

"A beautiful debut novel, sensitive and fragile . . . with naughty touches and satirical stings."

—*MAARIV*

WHERE
I AM

A NOVEL

DANA SHEM-UR

TRANSLATED FROM THE HEBREW
BY YARDENNE GREENSPAN

NEW VESSEL PRESS
NEW YORK

New Vessel Press

www.newvesselpress.com

Copyright © 2021 Dana Shem-Ur
First published in Hebrew as איפה שאני by Pardes Publishing
Translation copyright © 2023 Yardenne Greenspan

Library of Congress Cataloging-in-Publication Data
Shem-Ur, Dana
[Ayfoh She-Ani, English]
Where I Am/Dana Shem-Ur; translation by Yardenne Greenspan.
p. cm.
ISBN 978-1-954404-14-4

Library of Congress Control Number 2022944017
I. Israel—Fiction

PART I

DINNER
OR
ODE TO FOOD

APERITIF

WHEN Reut lay down on the bed, she knew there was no chance of getting real rest. Onlookers might speculate about a range of scenarios: a casual observer would see a woman on the cusp of middle age, well groomed, home after a dull day of work, physically and mentally exhausted. Her unusual posture—lying there obliquely on top of the blankets, shoes still on, light still on—was the obvious outcome of fatigue.

Another observer might analyze the scene more closely: rather than seeing merely a drained woman, they could intuit that Reut—now in her early forties—had carefully arranged herself in this position. The astute observer would have noted that this was someone who'd returned home two hours earlier, and had had more than enough time to undress, wash her face, put on soothing music and loose pajamas. But Reut had not done any of these things, the thought hadn't even crossed her mind. She had too much to do before her guests arrived.

It was Friday, a day Reut felt ambivalent about ever since she was a child: just as she'd yearned for the Sabbath (and its promise of rest), she dreaded its arrival (and its unfulfilled promise). At the end of each week, she was confronted by everything she hadn't accomplished, as if a testament to her personal inadequacy. Even matters as trivial as an out-of-place pillow would be enough to provoke a bout of self-flagellation as soon as she walked through the door.

That Friday, Reut came home in a particularly agitated state. Like a battery-powered toy, she began to frantically pace the apartment, performing a series of tasks that didn't necessarily contribute to the preparation of dinner. In the living room, she watered the plants and refolded the blanket draped over the armchair. In the kitchen, she reorganized the contents of the fridge. As she was peeing, she noticed that just one roll of toilet paper remained on hand. This observation sent her rushing to the bathroom cabinet to restock. Reut spent thirty-eight minutes in such activity before Jean-Claude's text message made her stop in her tracks:

"Got held up at work. I'll be right there, *chérie*!"

A mere hour and twenty-two minutes separated Reut from the moment the guests would arrive. In this short time span, she had to set the aperitif table, shower, put on a dress, and reapply her makeup. But her eyes were bothering her. They felt dry. And a pressure in her lower back joined a sudden trembling in her right eye. Slowly, her feet led her into the bathroom without any idea of what she planned to do there. Frozen in front of the mirror, she looked at her face. After close inspection, she turned off the light and dragged herself into the bedroom, as if that battery-powered toy were now on its last legs.

When she reached her bed, Reut had an hour and six-
teen minutes until the evening got fully under way, enough
time for a quick nap before attending to her hostess duties.
That calculation might have been accurate if she'd napped
only ten minutes, as she'd planned—not over an hour! How
did this happen?! The alarm clock, the shoes, the light—
they were all meant to ensure that she'd slip out of bed after
a brief respite with renewed vitality for such a special evening. In addition to their usual friends, another couple had
been invited that night—one that Jean-Claude referred to
as "important."

"Just a minute. Just one more minute . . . " Reut mumbled,
succumbing to the dimness behind her eyelids. But as she
said this, the rustling she'd heard in her sleep grew sharper.
Somebody was there. No—several people. Laughter rang out
nearby.

Her eyes opened. Startled, she grabbed her phone. A
quick glance at the screen.

"*Merde!*"

Leaping wildly out of bed, she approached the source of
the laughter with a terrified look on her face. She walked past
the hallway, past the living room. There was no more room
for doubt: the party was already underway in the kitchen.

A hesitant pause in the doorway, and then—an entrance
into the heart of the commotion. Taking in Jean-Claude, clad
in an apron, and then Stefan and Louise, standing together,
holding glasses of Chablis.

"*Bonjour*," Reut murmured. Then, in a tense voice directed at Jean-Claude: "The . . . the clock—I don't know what happened. Why didn't you wake me?"

Jean-Claude was in the middle of a tomato-slicing operation and seemed to be in good spirits. He abandoned his post, hands still wet, and glued his lips to hers, taking care not to get her dirty. "All's well, *chérie*," he reassured her, "I've taken care of everything. Ha! You should have seen yourself, how you slept! Poor thing . . . Let me pour you a glass of—"

"I'll be right back," she said, cutting him off. "All's well, quite well . . . " she murmured to herself, forcing a smile as she returned to the bedroom. But her heart kept racing in spite of her smile. She couldn't help but be suspicious of Jean-Claude's affectionate greeting after she'd left him alone to prepare for the evening. And how could he have allowed her to embarrass herself by letting her sleep so long? But Reut knew the guests didn't really care, especially not when it came to Stefan and Louise, a comparatively "inconsequential" couple. Then why this soaring tension? She rebuked herself for fretting, concluding there was no justification for her feelings. A marvelous dinner was about to begin, a dinner she herself had been looking forward to just that morning. But every expectation emerges from specific circumstances, and her eagerness about this evening had now all but disappeared.

They must be waiting for her! She had to get back to them, she couldn't keep torturing herself like this. She had to get rid of her anger. Reut ripped off her clothes and opened the closet, rummaging frantically through the underwear drawer until she found her pantyhose. Stuffing her legs into the hose, she stared vacantly into the closet, debating for several moments. She then pulled out the hanger with her favorite dress—her favorite not only because it was flattering, but also because it didn't constrain her from eating.

Reut slipped into the dress, won a quick battle with the zipper, and paused in front of the mirror on the closet door. After a brief analysis, she bent down toward the bottom drawer, pulled out a pair of black boots with chunky low heels, slipped them on, and continued into the bathroom. A quick reapplication of eyeliner and concealer, and she slammed the door behind her—louder than she'd planned—and hurried toward the living room.

Then, she paused.

She turned on her heels and stomped over to the kitchen, opened the fridge door, and looked inside vacantly. She came in here to get something, *but what?*

"Enough, Reut," she scolded herself. "This'll all be over in three hours."

A serene expression on her face, she vowed that from now until the end of the evening she would be in a wonderful mood. Marching into the living room, she finally joined her guests, initiating the traditional and obligatory French art of greeting.

When Reut walked into the living room, everyone was comfortably seated. The furniture was arranged in a horseshoe shape: two perpendicular sofas and one armchair to their left.

In the armchair was Antoine, Jean-Claude's longtime friend. Despite having met him numerous times, Reut could not shake her unpleasant first impression of him: an opinionated crime reporter for an independent journal who was convinced of his own intellectual superiority and lamented the failure of others to recognize it. Antoine was also a strikingly handsome man, well aware of his effect on others. It was no accident that he was always surrounded by an endless gaggle of women, all of them impressed with him, each hoping to be the one who would succeed in taming the wayward intellectual. Even Beatrice, his third and current wife, had tried her best, but like her predecessors, she seemed braced for defeat: Antoine could not be changed.

Beatrice sat on the end of the sofa closest to Antoine. Supervising. Of all his wives, Beatrice made the greatest effort to establish a friendship with Reut: phone calls, text messages, invitations to join her at this and that event. Beatrice worked at a small movie theater in the fifth arrondissement, but her true occupation was tracking down launches and cocktail parties. Always chasing and always alone—or at least that was what Reut had concluded. Otherwise, why the valiant effort to make friends?

To Beatrice's right, the sofa was occupied by Stefan and Louise. The least notable of Jean-Claude's friends. Pleasant enough. Stefan: a doctor of literature, an untenured professor at the Sorbonne, never quite attuned to university politics. Louise: a senior gynecologist at Pitié-Salpêtrière Hospital. The two had met as teenagers and had never parted. They seemed neither satisfied nor disgruntled with one another. The only thing Reut was certain about was that they no longer had sex.

Finally on the opposite side of the horseshoe, with their backs to Reut, were the distinguished guests sitting close together: Mikhail Grigoryev, the renowned Franco-Russian writer, and his newlywed wife, Ekaterina, or, more simply, Katya Grigoryev. It was easy to discern the couple's importance without even a glimpse of them: it was obvious from the other guests' postures. Like bits of metal drawn toward a magnet, they directed their full attention on the impeccable pair.

Jean-Claude, the only one standing, rushed to greet Reut as soon as he noticed her. Reut let him embrace her and looked at him affectionately. He seemed charmed by her, almost aroused.

"Tutu!" he called her by her nickname as he leaned toward the table to get her some wine. He'd come up with that term of endearment when they first started dating. "Tutu" was his intuitive way of adapting the throaty, complicated Israeli name pronounced Ré-oot into French.

As soon as Reut took hold of the glass, Jean-Claude carried on: "You know, Tutu, Mikhail just told me something that I think you'll find interesting . . ."

Reut smiled, surprised to find that her husband and the famous author were on a first name basis. Spontaneously, she turned her sunny expression toward Grigoryev, then returned her gaze to Jean-Claude, encouraging him with her eyes.

"*Alors*," he mumbled passionately, suddenly appearing flustered. Considering his next words, he reached for a bowl of olives he must have put together mere minutes before the guests had arrived, along with a bowl of spiced peanuts and another filled with chips. Swallowing an olive and tossing the pit into a smaller bowl nearby, he spoke: "*Ah-bien*, Mikhail's novel is going to be turned into a film!" Then, facing Grigoryev, "I'm really very curious to see how Mazzarini's going to do it. Adapting it into a movie, it's—well, if anyone can do it, it's Mazzarini. It's going to be wonderful!"

Reut smiled politely, sketching a surprised and enthusiastic expression on her face. "Which book is it?" she asked, sipping her wine.

"*In the Shadow of Darkness*," said Louise.

Jean-Claude interjected, "A great novel. You've read it, *chérie, n'est-ce pas?*"

Reut nodded and sighed softly. She'd always been amused by that expression—*n'est-ce pas?*—a non-question, really, an implication of the listener's compliance.

Jean-Claude was rightly impressed by rising-star Franco-Italian director Pierrot Mazzarini's bold move to film Mikhail Grigoryev's seven-hundred-page work. Adapting the non-linear, stream-of-consciousness novel, which follows its protagonist from birth to death in World War I, engendered both fascination and skepticism from the cognoscenti. Successful or not, it would be Mikhail Grigoryev's first book to be adapted into film, a notable achievement in and of itself. Jean-Claude was aware of this, which only heightened his eagerness to befriend the writer. In front of his guests, though, he tried to restrain his emotions. Adept at social maneuvers, he followed a guiding rule: converse with all others as your equals.

Though it was a deceptively simple rule, Jean-Claude believed it contained nuances that few people were able to implement. The greatest challenge was speaking to a person far from one's equal as if they were one's peer. This required an inner compass, the skill of balancing one's ego with one's respect for another. Without the former, Jean-Claude argued, the speaker would diminish themselves to the point of ridicule. But without the latter, one would be perceived as arrogant and an unworthy interlocutor. When Jean-Claude spoke to Grigoryev, he seemed to find perfect footing, toeing the line between the two modes: he built up his counterpart while making sure to express his own opinions with unmistakable confidence. This clever combination had found favor in Grigoryev's eyes from the first time the two had met—a mere two weeks before this Friday night dinner.

A fortnight ago, at one in the morning, Reut was roused by an incessant stroking at the back of her neck, the secondary purpose of which was to express affection, but the main goal of which was to pull her out of her slumber.

"Hmmm . . . What . . . I'm sleeping," Reut mumbled into the pillow.

"*Mon amour!* I'm so glad you're awake. You're not going to believe the night I've had!" Jean-Claude switched on the bedside lamp. The possibility of his listener dozing back to sleep while he relayed his news was unacceptable. As the light turned on, Reut—trapped and slow to react—realized she had to contend with a midnight onslaught of words and no possibility of escape. As soon as she murmured her defeat, Jean-Claude embarked on a detailed report of the night's events, analyzing from every possible angle the important connection he'd just made.

The key circumstance: Bernard de-Pestre, Jean-Claude's friend from the École Normale Supérieure, had returned to Paris after more than a decade holed up in Saint Petersburg with Marina Ostromohov, who'd eventually become Marina de-Pestre. The reason for the couple's return? An intellectual celebration! The publication of Bernard's debut novel, the philosopher having finally mustered the courage to fulfill his lifelong literary aspirations.

When Jean-Claude received an invitation to the event, he knew he'd have to attend and congratulate his old friend in person. But that afternoon he felt more tired than usual and informed Reut that he wouldn't stay long. He even promised to leave after two drinks and return home in time to join her and their nearly twenty-year-old son, Julian, for dinner.

But just as anticipations naturally change according to the situation, so do plans: How could Jean-Claude, when he made his promise, possibly imagine that this book launch would be attended by none other than Mikhail Grigoryev? How could he have guessed that the famous author was a close friend of the de-Pestres?

Obviously, Jean-Claude kept his cool when he figured this out. Bernard introduced the two and almost immediately left them alone at a corner table. It was there, after a minute or two of chitchat, that fortune favored Jean-Claude once more. He described this to Reut as "an amazing coincidence" (words she knew that, spoken by her, would have inspired his contempt).

"I don't even know how we got to talking about it," he remarked as his tale reached its conclusion. "I started telling him about the seminar I'm teaching, about Berdyaev. If you could have seen the look on his face when I mentioned that name! *Ber-dya-ev.* Turns out, he was greatly influenced by the man's existentialism, and—oh, there was even a moment when he started to quote a line from his book *Truth and Revelation!*" A faint clearing of the throat, and then—eyes still glimmering with the magic of it all—"Let me tell you something: he really is an extraordinary person, that Mikhail. Very sharp. We had a fantastic conversation."

Though Jean-Claude had been enormously fortunate that evening, his skeptical nature bested him. When he invited Grigoryev over for dinner a few days later, he never imagined it would actually happen. Jean-Claude maintained that same lack of faith even as he read Grigoryev's enthusiastic RSVP. Reading the text message once wasn't enough. It took three careful reads to convince Jean-Claude that the author truly intended to visit his home.

Once convinced, he became nervous, obsessively revising the menu, swapping main dishes in and out. Jean-Claude, who liked to think of himself as a talented cook or a culinary connoisseur, never took the dinners he hosted lightly. The success of a dish was tantamount to the success of the entire evening and the guarantee of intimacy among the guests. But even that wasn't enough for this particular Friday night dinner. The need to impress his visitors with his cooking had become almost secondary. The philosopher, who aspired to leave an indelible impression on Grigoryev, knew he would not achieve his goal simply by cooking well. The dishes would have to tell a story, move the writer, surprise him.

Jean-Claude thrived on the element of surprise. When Louise asked what they had to look forward to that night, he refused to share any information. Instead, he told her he had to return to the kitchen, apologizing to her and the other guests for his temporary absence.

The moment Jean-Claude left the room, Reut lost her relaxed demeanor. She was the only one now standing, glancing around with confusion, as if this weren't her own home. She tried to get a hold of herself, to express her opinion and pick up where Louise left off, but fell into silence once more.

Mikhail Grigoryev was watching her then. At some point, he stood up and offered her his seat, even though there was plenty of room on the sofas. Surprised by his offer and by the author addressing her at all, Reut thanked him but said that was unnecessary. Grigoryev shrugged while he remained standing. Clumsily, he reached for the bowl of chips, grabbed a handful, and chewed three of them in a loud rush. When the crunching was nearly complete, he turned to his hostess again, determined to start a conversation.

"Reut," he spoke in his deep voice, "you know, I used to have a very good friend from Israel. Nadav. It's incredible how alike you sound." A pause devoid of all thought, scooping up a few peanuts, and then, "Your accent is charming."

Reut smiled at the author wordlessly. It was an artificial smile, a kind Reut had deployed many times in her life. Sometimes she offered it with indifference, but mostly it was a result of a suppressed bitterness at that shibboleth—that imprecise pronunciation that revealed her foreignness, in spite of the nearly two decades she'd spent living in Paris.

"Jean-Claude tells me you're a translator, *n'est-ce pas?*"

"Indeed."

Contemplating, Grigoryev jutted out his bottom lip, raised his eyebrows, and nodded several times in succession. Then, almost inaudibly, "*Bien, bien . . .*"

"I—I translate from French into Hebrew. Prose, mostly."

"Ah."

"And English into Hebrew and vice versa, too."

"Ah," Grigoryev hummed again. Then, murmuring, "Sacred work, the craft of a translator . . . an incomparably important profession."

"Oh, she's so modest!" Beatrice's voice emerged. A voice that could draw anyone's attention. Sitting tall, legs crossed, right arm stretched all the way down her thigh, Beatrice turned to Grigoryev with a friendly, almost flirtatious tone. "She's also recently gone back to working on her doctoral dissertation. I don't know how she gets it all done! I truly admire her."

Beatrice meant well, but even knowing this, Reut couldn't help but take umbrage at the woman's glibness when it came to others' lives. Wary of anyone's tendency to form quick opinions about others, Reut volunteered little information about herself. After suffering many disappointments from people, her imagination had become quite creative, offering a wide array of interpretations about anything she might say. Had it not been for Beatrice, the conversation would have never turned to Reut's dissertation. How unsurprising that Beatrice brought it up! That constant need of hers to be liked was enough to send Reut into a rage. The logic of Beatrice's chatter seemed to rely on the assumption that as long as a comment sounded positive, it was worth making. And what could sound more positive than a person working on their dissertation? Perhaps even Reut would have interpreted the comment in a positive light if it had been made about some-one else. Perhaps even if it had been made about her at a different time in her life, if only the words "gone back" hadn't been part of it. She'd gone back to her dissertation.

"No need for admiration," Reut responded with a tight smile, not looking at Beatrice. As she said this, she walked over to the sofa where Katya was left sitting by herself, and leaned against the armrest. She felt the need to rest her body, even though she was no longer physically tired.

A brief silence filled the room. Reut restrained a hope for the return of prattle, but then, Grigoryev:

"What's your topic? If you don't mind my asking . . ."

"Oh, yes!" Beatrice chirped. "What are you writing about? I don't think you've ever told me."

At this question, Reut puffed out her chest and tried to conceal her nervousness through another forced smile. "I'm afraid I might bore you if—" she murmured, her eyes fixed on a random spot on the table. Then, looking up shyly, "I'm writing about the American Civil War. The question I'm examining is, well, oh, maybe another time we'll have an opportunity to—"

Reut reached toward the peanut bowl and grabbed a handful. Out of politeness, she didn't put them in her mouth right away, but kept her eyes on Grigoryev, waiting for him to speak.

But Grigoryev maintained his silence, only shifting his eyes. Soft, black pupils that seemed to plead with Reut to keep talking.

"Well, in short, what I'm writing about, what I'm concerned with, is the question, or, more accurately, the manner in which slave owners in the South understood what might be called 'the medieval knight myth.' In other words, how the romantic, aristocratic image of Southerners came into being, and, well, how it legitimized them, the Southerners, that is, to leave the Union. That's the—the gist of it, if you will."

"Very interesting!" Antoine squealed.

"Yes," Grigoryev confirmed, his thoughtful eyes half-closed. "Certainly. The question of myths has always been of special interest to me. But what—"

Grigoryev fell silent, jostling with his own thoughts in an attempt to arrange them into a cohesive sentence.

In the meantime, Reut dropped the peanuts, which were getting warm inside her fist, into a small dish and shot Katya a smile. As she took a seat beside Katya, Antoine's self-satisfied voice sounded once more.

"But, Reut, I must know, how did you even end up studying this subject? Isn't it somewhat esoteric?"

"How did I end up studying it? That's a very good question. How did I end up studying it . . . Unfortunately, I can't say I remember exactly. I . . . well, yes, perhaps I should have said I'm resuming the work I started back when I was still a young doctoral candidate at Columbia."

Aware of the aching nostalgia in her words and the bitterness in her voice, Reut trailed off, mortified. After that, she made sure to tinge everything she said with casual irony. "Wouldn't you say that's the advantage of esoteric subject matter? Forget about it for ten, twenty years, and it'll be right there waiting for you when you return, untouched by time—Oh! I'd like some, too—"

Reut leaned closer to the table, swiftly taking hold of her wineglass and offering it to Stefan, who was pouring pinot noir from a freshly opened bottle. While Stefan poured the wine, she carried on, "Well, as luck had it, during my first year at Columbia, a very special person joined the faculty: Jeffrey Sanderson. I can't remember why, but he came to Columbia on the brink of retirement. He'd been a professor at Berkeley his entire life, and then, three years before the end of his teaching career—Columbia. And, truly, if it hadn't been for him, then—He..." A pronounced sigh. Then, voice aflame, "Well, perhaps there is no point in talking about him, because he really is, he's one of those people, characters, you have to meet in person to understand. Anyway, he invited the whole class over to his place once a month, and always cooked us dinner! He never ordered in. We spent hours there, having discussions, listening to his stories."

Reut fell silent, her eyes glimmering. Distractedly, she gulped her pinot noir as if it were water, then carried on, a light tremble in her voice. "I've never met anyone with such passion for their work... so, yes, you might say I ended up studying what I do because of him. Thanks to him..."

The famous writer opened his mouth as if to speak, then must have thought better of it. During that brief pause, Jean-Claude appeared in the living room to report that he was in the final stages of the cooking process and would be joining the others shortly.

Once their chef departed, Grigoryev said, "So, this Sander—Sanderson, *oui*?—he was your advisor... And, forgive me, Reut, if I'm being invasive, but why didn't you complete your dissertation back then?"

Hearing this obvious question, Reut sighed and took her time. Telling Grigoryev how she accidentally got pregnant during her doctoral studies—and how Jean-Claude, who was about to complete his post-doc appointment, declared that he would not be postponing his return to

Paris—was something Reut had no intention of doing. A trite tale about yet another woman who sacrificed her prospects for the sake of her future husband. That's what they would think. They wouldn't be able to envision the dilemmas and fears that had flooded her, nor would they know what had preceded Jean-Claude in her life. They wouldn't be able to imagine the wonderful qualities she saw in him, the promise he held in her eyes: a tangible break with everything she'd known and despised. She loved him for his foreignness, and in spite of that foreignness. For the first time in a relationship, she felt herself not in the role of a judge but in the role of a student, discovering her life partner with cheerful curiosity.

When Reut finally responded to Grigoryev's question, her voice had a note of indulgence. "You're a writer. You must know as well as I do, or better, actually, that even when life seems most knowable, or perhaps especially when it does, it can still transform in a single moment, obliging you to change along with it."

"Aha," Grigoryev concurred, his preoccupied face bearing a secret. "And you know, let me tell you something else, Reut. This, this whole belief in structures, if you ask me, is erroneous to begin with. Structures are a fiction. *Vot.*"

Grigoryev was breathing heavily. He hadn't even noticed how that little word "*vot,*" which Russians often used to seal their statements, had snuck pervasively into his speech.

"What structures offer is not stability," he continued, "it's self-condemnation. And if you were able to let go of that . . ."

Excited, Grigoryev quickly placed his wineglass on the table. When his eyes rose back to meet those of his hostess, they appeared completely transformed, almost demonic.

"And I beg your forgiveness, Reut, for what I'm about to say, because I truly do applaud your research. But—how should I say this?—people's constant pursuit of a framework in which to situate themselves... that, that desperation to always guess the future... not only does it seem like a fiction to me, Reut, it's dangerous. Why not just die already and be done with it?"

While the question was left to echo in midair, Grigoryev bent down again to retrieve his wineglass. Then, without sipping from it, he continued, "So they have their sacred retirement fund. Their life insurance—I don't even know what that means, by the way. And how fanatically they hold on to those! People's entire life purpose has turned into a contract. But what are these contracts? Who in the venerable life insurance office would offer them financial indemnity for life? That eternal quest for some false security. Meaningless work contracts. People sell their lives for false contracts rather than truly live. *Vot.* It's—"

All of a sudden, Grigoryev fell silent. This sort of outburst was in no way typical of him. He didn't like to speak much, certainly not with strangers, and certainly not about such loaded topics. But if anything drove him mad, it was the abuse inherent in capitalism, and humans' ignorance of it.

Reut fixed her eyes on the author throughout his sermon, avoiding shifting in her seat, even though she was uncomfortable. The intensity with which he spoke surprised her and required her full attention. And she'd succeeded in concentrating, at least most of the time, her mind even supplying shards of ideas to bring up later. But then the speech reached its end, and the words abandoned her. All that remained was a feeling of oddness: bafflement at how what she said had led to the writer's discomfort.

Mute, she surreptitiously scanned the other listeners, trying to decode their thoughts on Grigoryev's opinion. During this brief period of observation, Antoine's face was the one that most intrigued her: severe, sour. No trace of his habitual smugness. Shortly thereafter, his tightly shut mouth opened to speak, allowing her to look at him again, this time openly.

In order to confront the guest of honor, Antoine chose to employ the art of French intellectual discourse, in which he was proficient. This art relied on clear, almost logical rules: comment A entailed comment B. The relationship between the two comments resembled a strategic gambit. "I completely agree with you, Monsieur," Antoine told Grigoryev, "and yet . . . "

Reut remained present for only a minute and a half of the critical aspect of Antoine's response. Following the journalist's weaving arguments, which said hardly anything of substance, was aggravating and mesmerizing in equal parts. Then she could bear it no longer: Antoine's theorizing tone made her stomach turn and her heart race. She had to get out of there.

Standing up abruptly, begging the others' pardon in a whisper, she headed toward the kitchen, having noticed Jean-Claude's prolonged absence. The moment she turned her back on the guests, her field of vision emptying of people and filling with things, she felt instant relief.

APPETIZERS

FROM the hallway, Reut recognized the music Jean-Claude chose to accompany his cooking. Eric Dolphy. An alto saxophonist, flutist, and bass clarinetist known for his meaningful influence on the evolution of free jazz.

For the past two weeks, Dolphy had sounded through their home every evening. That's how Jean-Claude always operated; there was almost nothing he didn't see as a peak to conquer. To him, even music wasn't a matter of simple listening. When he found a musician worthy of his tastes, he delved deep until a sufficient number of melodies became etched into his memory. Reut was a fan of Jean-Claude's obsessive nature so long as it didn't come at her expense.

As soon as she entered the kitchen, she hurried to the CD player to lower the volume of the saxophone, passing behind Jean-Claude, who didn't even notice her.

"Jean-Claude—"

"*Oui!*" He turned around with a start, his expression preoccupied, brown apron tied around his waist and oven mitts on his hands. He was in the crucial stage of extracting the bruschetta from the oven.

"One moment, Tutu," he barked, turning his back on her again.

A few seconds of standing in front of the oven; a few more seconds on his knees, watching alertly.

Then, Reut: "Jean-Claude—"

"*Chérie*, one moment! I'm asking you."

"I didn't say anything."

"Ah! *Dis-donc* . . ."

Reut glanced ruefully at the armada of pots and pans, then: "Jean-Claude, I—"

"One second."

Two seconds go by. Then, all of a sudden, Jean-Claude turned around, accusing eyes fixed on Reut. "Is something wrong?"

No, what the hell could be wrong, she wanted to respond, but was unable to get the words out. Her husband's senseless outbursts had a paralyzing effect on her.

"Mikhail," he interrogated, "did something happen? Did he say something?"

Silence.

"I'm asking you a question. Answer me."

"But what's going on with you?" Reut asked in a whispered shout, her lips barely moving.

No response.

Reut, the disciplinarian: "First of all, I want you to calm down. Are you calm? Can I talk now?"

"Ugh! Talk already. It's bad enough that some of the artichokes are ruined, but now the bruschetta is next! What is it? What? What's wrong?"

"I just came to check on you and see if I could help with anything. What else do you still need to do?!"

While Reut spoke, Jean-Claude ducked down toward the oven and nearly tore the door off. A thin plume of smoke rose out and dissipated in the air.

"Ah! *Dis-donc...*" he mumbled to himself. "Look at that. The artichokes were bad enough, but this—" His voice rose, directed at Reut now, "Tell them I'll be right there. There was—tell them there was a little issue with—no, just tell them I'll be right there. You know what, go ahead and seat them at the table. Yes, seat them. I'll be right there, *chérie...*"

Almost two whole minutes passed from the moment instructions were given until their execution. Even if Reut understood the importance of a quick turnaround, her feet were stuck to the kitchen floor, her eyes struggling to detach from Jean-Claude as he laid the bruschetta out on the counter. During those moments, all Reut wanted was to disappear, leaving Jean-Claude to handle things as he saw fit—most importantly, leaving him *alone*. She tended to treat their arguments as a kind of mystery. Even though they didn't fight often (Jean-Claude was categorically opposed to discussing things that bothered him, while Reut found it pointless to discuss with him things that bothered her), on the rare occasion that they did, Reut would face a black hole, struggling to recount what had led to the miserable outburst.

But something must have led to this, a voice of reason spoke within her. *He couldn't have spoken to me this way for no reason at all . . .*

This line of thinking, adhering to the logical chain of cause and effect, typically led Reut to conclude that she had missed something, that she was the one who had failed to correctly interpret the situation. This notion was sufficient to soothe her agitated state, which was, in fact, all she needed: a reason for her distress. The lack of a reason for suffering is often more painful than the suffering itself. And since access to Jean-Claude's locked-off (yet seemingly open) soul was denied to her, she usually tracked the source of the disagreement back to herself, rather than to him. Jean-Claude's mechanism of interpretation operated according to a different logic that led, however, to the same conclusion: he, too, assumed he had no other choice but to lay blame on Reut. Their interaction in the kitchen that evening was no different.

Reut finally tore herself away from the kitchen and walked to the living room. On the way, she mumbled a few words in Hebrew. When she reached her destination, she was pleasantly surprised: Antoine and Grigoryev's philosophical discussion was over!

Standing in the living room doorway, she paused to watch her guests unnoticed. Awaiting the right moment to speak, she suddenly grew impatient and walked quickly over to the sofas. Then, festively, she announced, "Jean-Claude asked me to let you know the food is ready. Shall we move to the table?"

She walked over to the exquisite wooden table and enjoyed a few moments of solitude. She had to plan out the seating arrangement for the evening. Life with her husband had taught her that she had to ensure two things: to not place Jean-Claude at the end of the table (the "desolation seat," meant for unimportant people), and to be sure to put Jean-Claude across from the Franco-Russian author (seating them side by side was out of the question; it would force an invasive intimacy). While maintaining these two conditions as the basis of the evening's success, all Reut had to ponder was properly situating the other guests. The challenge: devising a seating arrangement that would satisfy everyone, and—most importantly—prevent intense arguments. It took her less than forty seconds to reach a decision:

Seated near the wall with the wide window, from right to left: Mikhail Grigoryev, Louise, and Stefan. On the other side of Mikhail Grigoryev, in the "desolation seat"—Katya. Reut didn't like to seat women in the corner, but this time she made an exception. Her reasoning was that Katya wouldn't take an active part in the conversation anyway, because she lacked proficiency in French. On the other side of the table, Reut planned to seat Jean-Claude across from Grigoryev, and herself beside her husband. To her left, she placed Beatrice, in order to seat Antoine in the other "desolation seat," across from Katya.

Reut was pleased with the arrangement. Not only had she managed to avoid separating any of the couples, but she had also put sufficient distance between Antoine and the guest of honor.

Once the appetizers were on the table, the guests took their seats. Hiding their impatience, they awaited the cook's arrival so that they could finally embark on dinner and dinner conversations.

"Ooh-ooh! Jean-Clau-de!" Beatrice called out when their host appeared in the doorway. "Sit, sit! You've worked hard enough for us!"

Jean-Claude approached the dining table with a measured step, carrying an especially cherished bottle of wine.

Stefan, a wine aficionado, recognized the sublime bottle from afar. "*Oh la la!*" he cheered. "What's this pleasure you've brought us?"

"What . . . this?" Jean-Claude replied, giddy. "You might call this the 'bad boy' of the wine world. The finest rebel around."

The guests shared amused looks as Jean-Claude pulled the bottle opener from his pants pocket. While he carefully uncorked the wine, he explained with an intellectual air that this was an Italian vintage of the "Super Toscana" variety, famous for its boldness and sophistication.

"Super Toscana?" Beatrice marveled. "What did this wine do to be so super?"

Theatrically, Jean-Claude placed the decanter on the table, then poured the Italian wine into it. His celebratory expression was veiled by intense concentration. When he finished decanting the wine, he announced, "Wines like this need a little time to breathe, *n'est-ce pas?*"

While it was breathing, ceremony obliged the diners to listen to an introduction of what they were about to enjoy:

"I've been saving this marvelous bottle right here in my *cave* for over a decade," he announced jubilantly.

"A smart purchase," Stefan said solemnly.

"What you're about to taste is a Grattamacco by ColleSammari. 1999 harvest."

A pause of reflection, then: "Pardon, no, no: ColleMassari. A 1999 Grattamacco by ColleMassari. I must admit I'm a bit excited."

A clearing of the throat, then with renewed confidence: "You asked why 'super,' Beatrice? Well, the reason is simple! In the 1970s, Tuscan winemakers protested the strict wine production regulations enforced in the Chianti region. Well, 'protested' is not the right word. Let's just say they didn't completely honor them. I won't burden you with the statute for the grape varieties that must be included in a Chianti. For our purposes, what you should know is that those winemakers were forbidden from using the name 'Chianti' on their labels, which didn't help sales. And, well, that's how they got their unofficial name: Super Tuscany."

"*D'accord*!" said Beatrice. Like many Parisians, she added an unconscious, soft sigh after her "*d'accord*." When Reut first learned French, it took her a while to realize that this sigh was not a gasp, but rather an expression of marvel or agreement.

"And what was truly 'super'," Jean-Claude continued, "is that contrary to what the conservatives believed, these wines proved that a small-scale rebellion pays off. These days, they're considered the finest wines in the world. Enough talk. Now—"

Jean-Claude took hold of the decanter's neck, swirled it for a few seconds, then said, "Shall we?"

Reut thought that Jean-Claude could have spared the guests the long gastronomic speech. Though she had no difficulty predicting where his introduction would lead. Indeed, for the next twenty minutes, all the happy bunch could talk about was the Grattamacco, the different sensations it inspired in them, as well as the memories: memories of other wonderful wines they'd sampled in the past, whose flavor had etched itself into their souls. Reut couldn't identify the exact moment when she stopped relishing these sorts of discussions and began to feel revolted by them.

In her first years with Jean-Claude, she was charmed by wine conversations. Her fervor was natural. In her life prior to their relationship, wine was nothing more than a small bottle in her eyes, something that could either accompany a meal or be absent from it. It didn't enjoy a place of honor on her table, let alone the near-magical powers Jean-Claude and his friends attributed to it. Thanks to them, she was introduced to a practically foreign language, and with her growing familiarity with terms such as "full-bodied," "perfumed," or "astringent," Reut not only expanded her vocabulary, but—as when learning any language—she also acquired a new world of experiences. A world in which all the symbols that once seemed so nebulous now took on profound meaning, flavor, and aroma.

Under Jean-Claude's tutelage, Reut felt as if she'd gone from being an outside onlooker to an initiate in a secret society. As if she'd spent years visiting museums yet had a limited view of canvases, shapes, and colors, until the day a generous expert shared insights that opened up a broader appreciation of art. Reut felt as if she'd been lucky enough to contemplate Malevich's *Black Square* or Duchamp's *Fountain* without seeing just a polygon or a urinal, but rather gumption and rebellion. She felt as if she'd never again find pastoral pleasure in van Gogh's wheat fields, but only despair and lonesomeness. The words heightened her sensitivities, and it was riveting and thrilling.

"—ut? Re-u-ta!"

"*Oui?*" Reut was startled, disoriented.

"Reut, *chérie*," Beatrice said, "is everything all right?"

"Yes, I—"

But before Reut could finish, Beatrice turned to Grigoryev to share her impressions of their hostess. "You'll see, she's always like this, head in the clouds. If I didn't know her, I might have thought we were boring her!"

"No, of course not! It's . . . " Reut trailed off. "Forgive me, I'm just a little concerned about—nothing. It's nothing." Narrowing her eyes, Reut appeared as if she were still pondering that little bit of nothing. Then, in a higher register, she asked, "Julian. Wasn't he supposed to be home by now?"

"No, *chérie*," Jean-Claude sighed. "I told you, he texted me that he's studying with a friend. He'll be back in time for dessert."

Reut knew that Jean-Claude had told her no such thing, but she had no patience to linger on the subject. All of a sudden, all she could think of was her hunger. She glanced at her plate, which was nearly bare. It was time to enjoy some appetizers.

The table was overflowing with a rich selection of fine foods. Almost all the dishes were vegetarian, to accommodate Katya's lifestyle. Jean-Claude had conducted some research about the couple's culinary preferences ahead of time. The menu was eclectic, an indication of the cook's curiosity: at the center of the table, in a wide, blue ceramic tray, the nearly burnt bruschetta was neatly arranged alongside a pair of baguettes to enrich the offering of carbohydrates; alongside the tray was a bowl of artisanal hummus he'd bought in Le Marais, extra-virgin first-press olive oil, and balsamic vinegar; on the right end of the table, near the Grigoryevs, was a bowl of fluffy mashed potatoes, surrounded by small dishes of steamed vegetables. Next to the broccoli was a challenging dish Jean-Claude had decided to try for the first time that night: tomatoes stuffed with foie gras and chanterelles. On the left end, beside the bruschetta and in the same Italian vein, a tray of fried artichokes—a traditional dish favored by Roman Jews that Jean-Claude had learned from his friend and colleague Daniel Finzi and of which he was especially proud. Next to the artichokes, close to Beatrice and Antoine, was a deep bowl of Greek salad and a spinach and goat cheese quiche that Jean-Claude had purchased early that morning.

Focused on eating, Reut hadn't noticed the first collective hush that had fallen since the beginning of the evening. The hush resulted not from any lull in conversation, but rather of each diner's obedience to their rumbling stomachs. It was Grigoryev, the fastest to polish off his plate, who broke the silence.

"Oh, where's the challah?" he asked, as if just recalling a question of utmost importance.

"Challah?" Jean-Claude sputtered through a mouthful of artichoke.

"Oh, no, I'm not observant," Reut explained, "and Jean-Claude is—"

"Katyushka's family is traditional," Grigoryev said, cutting her off. "I'm very fond of your Friday night ritual."

"*Bien*," Jean-Claude murmured. "*C'est bien.*"

Grigoryev paid no heed to Jean-Claude's mumbling. His mind wandered back to a question Louise had asked about the book he was now writing, which led to a conversation that lasted several minutes. At the same time, a few other side conversations harmoniously played out: some banter between Reut and Antoine, a fervent discussion between Stefan and Beatrice (who raised her voice significantly in an attempt to surpass Louise's volume). Those small-scale exchanges quickly expanded to include three people, with a few individuals left out on their own. Meanwhile, Jean-Claude jumped restlessly from one conversation to the next, struggling to keep engaged. He was mostly preoccupied with his discovery of Katya's Jewishness—a fact he'd overlooked in his research on the couple.

Raised Catholic, and an avowed atheist and existentialist since coming of age, Jean-Claude could not imagine a life revolving around religious ritual. What he found most vexing, as he'd often told Reut, was the belief that a series of practices could accord a person their life's meaning; the thought that, from birth onward, a person methodically strives to detach their life from their thinking self, from their dreaming self—a wish to redeem one's soul by conforming to the herd. When Reut heard him make these kinds of statements, she would nod and listen patiently until he finished. What good would it do to voice her opinion on the matter, or even share her puzzlement at the amusing, almost ironic gap between his field of academic research (religious philosophy) and his critical view of spiritual life?

PLAT PRINCIPAL

Reut quickly joined Jean-Claude in the kitchen. She knew that it went against French custom to leave the guests on their own, but she felt a deep discomfort that wouldn't let her sit still. She had to get up and busy herself with something. The same distress that had plagued her earlier that evening was thickening, dulling her senses. Everything she saw, heard, tasted—it was all bland. She'd been in that interior haze so often, present yet not truly there at meals and conversations. Much like the way she listened to music, Reut absorbed the overall melody, catching only bits and pieces of the individual words.

Against the backdrop of Antoine's discordant tune, Reut pondered her many problems. One moment, she was fretting over her transatlantic phone call with Shira, a close but often irksome childhood friend from Israel, and the next, she was irritated by her publisher—what was with that email scolding her for "errors" in her translation? Her mind reeled onward, toward other problems, and finally another one entered her mind just seconds before she stepped into the kitchen.

"Tutu!" Jean-Claude called out, recognizing the ticking of her heels even from the hallway. "Come in here for a moment please."

"What's wrong?" she asked.

"Oh, good, you're here! I was just—" He fell silent, and Reut noticed his crooked pose over the stove.

"I'm glad you're here," he said, turning quickly away from her, returning to the stove. "I need your help."

Reut nodded, awaiting instructions. But her previous desire to be given a task was now replaced with a desire to leave the room.

"Are you still there?!" he growled.

"Yes."

"Then why aren't you saying anything?"

"*Mon Dieu*, will you just tell me what you want?"

"So what I—just one moment..." Jean-Claude took a sip of the stew, lowered the heat a touch, then carefully placed the wooden spoon back on the counter and turned to face her. "It turned out wonderfully. Want a taste, *chérie*?"

"No, thank you."

"What did I want? Oh! The wine." Jean-Claude walked quickly toward Reut. "Tutu, if you could just bring them the—one second... I know! Oh, and if you could maybe also—ah, never mind. We'll do that later. Just the wine. If you could go to the *cave* and grab the 2014 Saint-Émilion Château Troplong Mondot." Jean-Claude pronounced every syllable as if to avoid any possible confusion. "It's in the far right corner of the cabinet. You can't miss it. Saint-Émilion. Troplong Mondot. 2014. *D'accord*?"

Reut gave Jean-Claude a piercing look. "*D'accord.*"

Jean-Claude stared at her, thinking. "And if you could

just give it to Stefan to uncork. I don't want any mishaps with that bottle."

Reut kept her gloomy eyes on Jean-Claude. Then, without even noticing, she closed them briefly. When she opened them again, she huffed and left the kitchen. But before she could take seven steps, Jean-Claude called out again.

"Tutu . . ."

Reut paused.

"*Chérie*. Come in here please."

Reut turned around suspiciously, retracing her steps. When she faced Jean-Claude, they stared at each other in silence. He saw the expression of an iceberg. She saw a face full of care.

"What's wrong?" he asked. "You look strange. What happened?"

Reut hesitated. She hated being called "strange." "Everything is fine," she said, offering the requisite response.

Jean-Claude followed suit. "No, something's wrong." Pleadingly, he asked, "What's the matter, *chérie*?"

"It's nothing. It's, it's nothing, just Shira. I'm worried about her. Her father, you know, he's in the hospi—"

Jean-Claude placed both hands on her arms before she could finish the sentence. A light smile on his lips, he watched her, tightening his grip as he filled his chest with air. Then, just like Reut had predicted: a hug. But it was a different hug than she'd expected. It was a rough, somewhat aggressive hug, a kind that didn't necessarily seek to comfort. Crushed between his arms, Reut couldn't help but wonder at how quickly Jean-Claude's groin hardened against her. As his breath grew heavy and quick, she tracked his gentle, ardent movements with indifference.

A kiss on the neck. A long one.

No response from Reut.

Jean-Claude continued to hug her, hard, arms spreading along her narrow back. They moved quickly now, up and down, fanning his flames. All of a sudden, his hands paused on her rear. They gripped it roughly, sculpting it, becoming intimate with the flesh. Reut let out a sigh of pleasure. Jean-Claude added his own.

"*Chéri*." She pushed him away with a smile. "What's come over you?"

In response, Jean-Claude put his lips to her neck. Then he whispered, "*J'ai envie de toi . . .*"

His lips burrowed into her neck again. She mumbled something. He should stop. She moaned gently.

"Enough, *chéri*, have you gone mad?" Giggle. "What are you—oh . . . hmm . . . The guests, what about the—" A deep breath, another sigh of pleasure. "This isn't—what's with you, the food, the guests may be here any . . . enough. Jean-Claude . . . stop, let me go . . . Jean-Claude!"

Reut pulled away from Jean-Claude's persistent touch. Her body had certainly been aroused, but her mind had determined this was not an appropriate time for intimacy, even if only playful. Jean-Claude knew very well that one of the guests could step into the kitchen at any moment. Their desire was only stoked by the shared knowledge that it could not be fulfilled.

Reut left Jean-Claude looking like a lion that had just lost its prey, and hurried out of the kitchen. She noticed she'd gone beyond the point of slightly tipsy, losing a smidge of her self-control. Before she had a chance to turn right toward the *cave*, her feet carried her into the bathroom. There, she turned on the light and pressed her head against the mirror, turning it left and right, then stretched her neck as if sketching an imaginary brushstroke on the glass. Her left hand joined the dance, caressing her neck and grazing her chin sensually.

She felt her body still warm, yearning, then she panicked. What was wrong with her? The guests. Oh, and the wine! She'd forgotten all about it! She glanced in the mirror one last time, sprayed herself liberally with perfume, and left the bathroom, bathed in the deep scents of vanilla and jasmine. A seed of anger sprouted within her: there was something infuriating about Jean-Claude's display of desire in the kitchen.

For a while now, Reut had noticed a crucial change in his sexual urges. Too often, he seemed to need a backdrop of friends in order to play the part of a husband who had not grown tired of his wife after so many years together. Once again, Reut couldn't help but compare this moment to all those lonely nights when Jean-Claude would come home late, preoccupied, stingy with his affection. When he initiated at night it was with a sort of languid monotony. And yet, he initiated more often than she did, and when he did, everything went along more or less as it should. She kept reminding herself of this, encouraging her rational mind to take over.

Again, logic pushed her to rebuke herself. She had to learn to avoid the merry-go-round of bitter thoughts that caused her to wallow in self-pity. What was so wrong about Jean-Claude getting excited about her around his friends, when he was in high spirits, feeling happy and loose? And what was so unusual about him being tired in the evenings and not showering her with affection at any given moment? It was certainly possible she'd have felt the same things with any other man, she reminded herself, hoping for some unattainable harmony, and plagued with insecurity when it never arrived.

"Tutu!" Jean-Claude cried, trudging heavily, focused on the stainless-steel pot in his arms, "Make some room over there please—right there."

Reut quickly fulfilled her husband's request, but Jean-Claude realized he'd forgotten the trivet and asked her to hurry up and grab it, along with another pot from the kitchen.

When she reappeared, Jean-Claude asked with delicate mystification: "Where'd you disappear to earlier?"

The guests had by now leisurely reconfigured themselves. The fact that Stefan and Katya were now sitting beside each other forced the others to change seats: Antoine quickly upgraded himself away from the desolation corner. Reut sat down across from him, mere moments before Beatrice crushed the remaining half of her cigarette and gracefully carried her body to the table. Grigoryev did not hurry after her. Instead, he remained standing by the window for a few moments longer, indulging in tobacco and the howling of cold wind out on the street. When the writer returned to the table, Jean-Claude's culinary address could officially begin. It was much shorter than the Grattamacco speech, but no less ceremonial:

"I must admit that I'd had quite a dilemma when it came to tonight's main dish. Ha, ha. An overabundance of inspiration can sometimes be just as paralyzing as a lack of inspiration! But ultimately I felt certain about what I wanted to make for you all tonight. And, by the way, the idea came to me completely by chance."

As he spoke, Reut felt her body heating up from the wine again. She watched her husband with curiosity, examining his features. For moments here and there, she was able to join the group of listeners in spirit, not as Jean-Claude's wife, but as a woman observing an unfamiliar man, analyzing him, isolating his different qualities with her eyes: yellowish-tan skin, wide, strong hands, bright almond-shaped eyes, a single dimple on his right cheek, a black button-down revealing a patch of chest. His lips sucking on her neck, her body trembling— the memory of the kitchen returned to her, enlivening her. As soon as it appeared, the memory dissipated, bringing back the oh-so-familiar Jean-Claude, her husband. She listened.

"The *France Culture* radio program, the one in the afternoon, ran an interview with Tarnowski, a very controversial writer in Poland nowadays. So he talked a little bit about the, his childhood, which reminded me of the fabulous soup I ate in Poland a few years ago. You might already be guessing the dish I'm talking about . . ."

His audience awaited the big reveal.

"Borscht, of course! And it was the most delicious borscht I've ever had. Unbelievable! I was at a, a phenomenology conference in Warsaw a few years ago. One night, they took us to a small restaurant, a kind of inn. It was on a main street in town, but we could have just as easily missed it. An unsophisticated place, unassuming. Just come in and eat. That sort of place. So what I'm—we'd better start eating before the soup gets cold—no, but, just one moment. Let me tell you a bit about the dish, for those of you unfamiliar with it."

Jean-Claude looked at Grigoryev like a child seeking his father's permission to speak.

"*Pardon*," he continued, clearing his throat. "Well, borscht is a traditional Slavic dish, hundreds of years old. To this day, it is still unknown exactly when and where it was invented. What's wrong with me? I forgot the most important thing! One second, I'll be right back."

Within a minute, Jean-Claude ran to and from the kitchen not once, but twice. The first time, he brought a bottle of fine Kyiv-made vodka and some shot glasses. The second time, he carried in a tray with eight little bowls of crème fraîche, along with slices of Russian black bread. Without all these, he warned, there was no point in having borscht!

Following the chef's orders, Reut dolloped a little crème fraîche into her soup bowl but had to stop eating after three heaped spoonfuls. To her surprise, even after having waited through Jean-Claude's long speech, the borscht was still hot enough to burn her tongue. After a brief pause, she took hold of the spoon again. Between the soup and the wine someone had poured for her (when and by whom? she hadn't noticed), Reut filled her stomach swiftly, never pausing until her bowl and glass were nearly empty. A thick slab of beef was lying at the bottom of the bowl like a slumbering beast. She looked at it, hiccupped, grabbed her spoon and hiccupped again, rushing to sip uncomfortably from her water. The spoon pierced the soft hunk, splitting it into halves, then quarters, as if Reut were planning to share her dish with an imagined toddler version of Julian.

She fished out one of the chunks and slipped it into her mouth, swallowing without chewing. A mighty cough threatened to erupt from her throat. She could feel it, a tornado intensifying inside of her, and she closed her eyes and battled the storm, searching for air. The tiniest cough emerged. She raised her head victoriously and pushed the bowl lightly away. Now she tried to listen to the conversations around her. It was an honest, though pointless, endeavor. After a few moments of respite, her discomfort began to bubble up once more.

She grabbed a piece of dense black bread. As her teeth were grinding away, she ripped off a second piece in preparation. Then she stood up, searching for the bottle of Troplong Mondot that had drifted far away from her. With an apologetic expression, she tried to signal to Grigoryev to pass it her way, but he was entirely absorbed in his conversation with Louise. Reut was awash with frustration and helplessness. She thought she could feel the others' judging looks without daring to verify her hunch.

"Stefan . . . Stefan . . ." she called softly, eyeing the bottle awkwardly.

"Ah-*oui*!" Stefan jumped up. "Of course." She thanked him and exchanged two or three words with him before sipping her wine. She reached toward the pot of soup and refilled her bowl halfway. But before she could enjoy it, she again felt that intense tightness in the chest.

INTERMEZZO
(DIGESTION AND CIGARETTE BREAK)

INHALE, exhale, mindful actions. When a modicum of relief took effect, Reut got up from her seat like someone reprieved from an asthma attack. She excused herself without looking up and marched to the bathroom, wilted and winded, her head diving into her hands. She didn't turn on the light and remained immobile on the toilet. Her chest still hurt, and now her lower belly did as well. The sensation of needles pricking her from the inside relentlessly. Reut was very familiar with those pinpricks, which were nothing like a normal stomachache. They plagued her time and again, as if they wanted something from her—perhaps to drive her insane? How else could she explain these mysterious attacks?

The doctors had utterly ignored the problem, and Reut was left with no choice but to accept the pricking as an inescapable part of her life. Dr. Silvansky, their family physician, was the first person she'd consulted, and the first person to let her down. Reut trusted him, and he barely pretended to offer a solution during her visit. Everything was in working order, he determined flatly. At worst, the culprit was an imbalanced diet. *Imbalanced*? she protested. How could that be? She tried to explain to the doctor that no one was more balanced than she was when it came to food, but all he could provide was a referral to a dietitian and the gift of a listening ear.

When Reut met with the dietitian, her intuition proved to be true: her eating habits, she was informed, were perfectly balanced, and could not be the cause of her pain.

Reut knew this verdict ought to bring some relief. How could she not be pleased when two doctors informed her that her body was in perfect health? But while the dietitian spoke, all Reut could think about was the violent pricking that had started up just then. She hesitated to share this with the dietitian. It was her word against that of two specialists, and she feared they'd view her pain as hysterical. Reut herself wondered if that might be the case. A business card the dietitian gave her implied that it was certainly possible. "He's a great psychotherapist," said the dietitian, pointing at the card. "He'll help you deal with the stress."

The consultation with the dietitian had taken place about three years before this Friday night dinner. Since then, as often happens when one takes an interest in a certain subject, Reut had been exposed to huge amounts of information on the effects of mental stress. She discovered that the variety of symptoms was nearly infinite! Her own personal research made her aware of an "unnatural" tension in her front teeth, her "unnatural" hair loss, her "unnaturally" quick pulse, and her occasional "unnatural" eyelid twitches. Once Reut learned about all of these phenomena, she developed a superhero's heightened sensitivity toward her own body— noting every change, every shift, every part that felt slightly different than it had the previous day. She kept these changes from Jean-Claude, as well as the worry they inspired in her. From the moment she accepted the fact that the source of these symptoms—her stress—was incurable, she found no point in sharing her experiences with him. She predicted he would respond with indifference or judgment, and foresaw difficulty in dealing with either.

Reut got up from the toilet slowly, flushed, opened the door, and jumped back, startled. Stefan was standing there.

"Stefan! Have you been here long?"

"Not too long. I was waiting for you to come out."

"You were waiting? Why didn't you say anything? I was—"

"I . . ." He fell silent.

Reut's heartbeat was still elevated from the surprise. She didn't know what to say. A few seconds later, she asked, "Is everything all right?"

"Yes, yes."

Reut was baffled by the sudden joy that had taken over Stefan. She smiled. "I suppose you need the bathroom, so I'll—"

"Ah-*oui*!" he cut her off. Then, his voice deeper: "*Oui* . . ."

"Okay, I'll go back to—"

"Um, Reut—" Stefan's arm grabbed hers.

She looked at his face, then at his hand, which, to her astonishment, continued to hold on to her. Stefan stared at her longingly.

Reut's pupils danced nervously. Suddenly, she let out a laugh. "Is something the matter?"

"That's what I was going to ask."

"Stefan—" She released herself from his grip. "I, I don't understand what—"

"Reut," he said, seeming to derive erotic pleasure from pronouncing her name. "You know you can talk to me. You know that, right?"

"I . . ." she mumbled, scrunching her eyebrows.

"Are you not feeling well?" he asked, drawing closer.

"Umm, ah . . ." she stuttered. "Why—"

"You disappeared," he said. "I noticed before that you weren't . . . feeling well. And then, then you disappeared." Stefan drew out the words, treating each pause with respect. His intimation of a smile was at odds with what he was saying. He could use any sentence to disguise what he was actually telling her through his facial expression.

"I'm fine," she said, her eyes darting all around.

"Good. I was worried about you." Stefan's smile faded at once. A chameleon face, alternately ingratiating, then utterly serious. He fixed his eyes on her. It had been clear to her from the start of this interaction that it might reach this point, but everything happened so fast, too fast for her brain to process. It was as if she were witnessing a fragile object crash to the floor and was helpless to prevent its fall.

Stefan told her she was beautiful and placed his hand against her warm cheek. Perfect! Now she could no longer pretend she had misread his intentions.

"Stefan!" She pulled away, her eyes reproachful.

Her look made him pull himself together. Once again, she was facing the polite Stefan who concealed his sexual frustration. He apologized fervently, blamed the wine, claimed that all he wanted was to check on her. Suddenly he seemed dour and miserable. She assured him that she understood, though in truth she did not at all and was suffering intense discomfort. She encouraged him to go into the bathroom, and he obeyed.

As she made her way back to the dining room, Reut's face was expressionless. But a shiver of shock and nausea took hold of her body. *Stefan.* She didn't see that coming! A nervous guffaw escaped her. Then her face went stony again, but heated up at once. Her eyes swelled, and she paused, holding her hands over them for a few seconds. *Don't be ridiculous. Everything's fine. Everything's fine.* She patted her face lightly, making sure no dampness remained.

Then she entered the lion's den.

Reut accompanied her guests into the living room to relax before dessert. After a few moments of serene conversation, the second silence of the night took hold, testament to the harmony that had developed among the diners. Reut, cross-legged on the end of the sofa, watched them halfheartedly, blurrily taking in their limp expressions. Some of their faces seemed like a window into their daydreams, while others seemed translucent, without a single thought. Each person was simply sitting on the sofa, digesting and enjoying some quiet. And then the silence was broken with the same ease that had created it, without anyone noticing. Here a delicate request for a cigarette, there a remark on the gray weather, then the chitchat resumed before a key suddenly jingled in the front door.

The sound was accompanied by Reut's liberated laugh, which rang out through the living room, washing away any strain and sadness. The door opened and in walked her son, Julian, who had kept his word to be home for dessert. When Reut raised her head and looked at him, again her laughter took on new dimensions, awakening the guests' curiosity camouflaged by concern. She could have just as easily started crying as laughing. Everything was so ridiculous—the people around her, she herself.

Between bursts of laughter, Reut pleaded with Julian to join her and the guests, but he dismissed her with the excuse that he'd had a long day and promised to be back in a little while. A surprise met him upon his return: Mikhail Grigoryev was seated on the sofa in all his glory. Julian, who liked to proclaim to his friends that Grigoryev's style of writing wasn't his taste, could not help but be moved by the man's presence. In an instant, he transformed from a principled man of letters—previously determined not to attend the meal so as not to play a part in his father's cult of personality—into a charmed, starstruck boy. Hurrying toward the sofas, he embarked at once on the double-kiss ceremony, rushing first through the familiar pairs of cheeks. When he reached the famous author, he made sure to conceal any trace of excitement. Much like his father, Julian had an inner scale that allowed him to keep a measured balance in public.

And yet, when he approached beautiful women, Julian often lost his cool. Though he felt fully in control as he conversed with them, he was completely unaware of the passion that glittered in his eyes. And so, when it came time to exchange kisses with Ekaterina, Julian as usual was unable to conceal his marvel at the being revealed to him—one who could sit so nobly on the sofa, one who could offer her cheeks so daintily for his kisses. So many details in just a few brief glimpses:

First, the magnificent way Katya smelled (was it her neck? her hair?), her cat eyes (what color were they? he hadn't noticed), her full lips, painted with a shiny crimson lipstick, and, of course (to his joy), the deep plunge of her white dress, with no bra underneath. From the moment Julian noticed the neckline, he made sure to keep his eyes on hers, though the image of it kept floating in his mind while they spoke.

"*Enchanté*. Very nice to meet you," he said, adjusting his stance.

Katya smiled with closed lips and returned the greeting.

"*Pravda, ochin priatna*," he said, in Russian this time. "*Ya*, Julian. *A vi*?

"Ekaterina Mamanof Grigoryev. *Ochin priatna*."

Julian's sudden switch to Russian surprised Katya, causing her smile to widen so much that her lips parted, gracefully revealing her teeth. She turned to Julian and asked him a question in Russian that he could barely decipher. He apologized, admitting that he wasn't yet fluent enough to carry a conversation. Reading and writing were "no problem," he emphasized, then explained that as part of his Russian studies at the École Normale Supérieure he focused on reading eighteenth- and nineteenth-century texts. He told her that he was currently working on a paper in which he examined Marcel Proust's influence on Vladimir Nabokov.

At this, the smile around Katya's eyes vanished abruptly. Indifferently, she said, "Interesting. *Interiyesna.*"

"What? *Shto interiyesna?*" Grigoryev interjected.

Reut watched the author surreptitiously. It was obvious to her he hadn't been listening to a word Julian had said. Beneath his expressionless face, she thought she recognized irritation or despair, she wasn't sure which.

"Shall we move on to desserts?" she proposed gently, thinking that sweets would do Grigoryev good, that they would do her good. The evening was almost over.

CHEESE AND DESSERT

A FEW dirty glasses in her hands, Reut asked Julian (*ordered him*, to take his word for it) to join her in the kitchen and help bring out the desserts. She told him she wanted to discuss something while they were at it.

In the hallway, Julian: "What is it?"

"One second," she said, "Come."

Reut sped up, rushing into the kitchen like a woman possessed. Julian, who had been dawdling after her, paused in the doorway and watched her scurry between the fridge and the cabinets. So much to do!

Julian couldn't exactly say why, but something about the way his mother moved seemed sad to him, even pathetic. But he noticed she was dressed well, recognizing Reut's black winter dress, which she'd already worn to a number of events. His gaze shifted from the dress to her hair and the somewhat tired and cumbersome way it rested on her shoulders, then onward to the blush rouging her cheeks. That flushed hue seemed too intense to have been the result of a cosmetic product. He imagined it had to do with the wine, and wondered how much she'd had to drink.

Julian grew tired of examining his mother's appearance

and became impatient. Why did she tell him to come? Why must he stand there like an idiot?

"*Bien*!" he announced. "I'm going."

"Julian, *chéri*!" she cried. "Come here for a moment please. Stand by the coffeepot for a few minutes. Tell me when you see small bubbles—before the water boils, remember? When you see small bubbles."

Wary of a confrontation, Julian obediently manned his station.

"Wasn't there something you wanted to talk about?"

"What's that, *chéri*? Reut called. She was concentrating on slicing a blueberry tart—Beatrice and Antoine's contribution to the dinner.

"*Mon dieu*! You said you wanted to talk about something, didn't you?"

"Yes!" she cried with exaggerated cheerfulness. "There was that . . . I wanted, umm . . . I'll remember in a second, *chéri*. Why don't you tell me about your day?"

"It was fine. Well, Mom, I've got things to do."

"One second—" She abandoned the tart and returned to the stove. She noticed the water bubbling inside the coffeepot and pushed Julian aside to turn down the heat. "Why didn't you tell me?!"

"Ah! It, it only just now—"

"Don't go. Just give me a moment to finish making the coffee and—Where's the—"

Julian fell silent and stayed planted in place. His eyes were trained on his mother's hands as she filled the pot with a few heaping spoonfuls of coffee and stirred the grounds. Then she invited him to sit beside her at the table while the Turkish brew was heating up. Still silent, Julian trudged over. In an instant, his arms were lying on the table, folded to form a square for his heavy head to rest upon.

"Are you tired?" she asked, managing to restrain her familiar plea for him to sit up straight.

"So tireeeeeddd . . . "

"Why? What did you do today?"

"I told you, I had a good day."

"I didn't ask how it went. I asked what you did."

Julian sat up and in a monotone started to bring his mother up to date on his different activities, focusing on his academic assignments. Reut listened at first, trying to train her entire being on her son. But she soon found herself battling to concentrate. Without even noticing, her attention began to wander from the words he said to his tone of voice, or, to be exact, to Julian's oh-so-French inflection. This was not the first time she'd noticed it, but each time it surprised her anew. In these moments, all she could hear was a foreign melody, an unending tale woven by a man with an impeccable Parisian accent, who just so happened to be her son, but could have just as easily been a stranger. Sometimes Julian sounded to her like a Truffaut film character. Other times, when she listened in on his social interactions, he seemed to play unnatural word games, creating mutations out of the very language that she had worked so hard to learn and internalize. Either way, Reut couldn't help but be impressed by the lightness with which the words tumbled from his mouth, the spontaneity, the way in which they preceded—or at least over-lapped with—his thoughts. Reut listened to him, her son—her son who thought in French, loved in French, laughed in French, and hurt in French, all of those realities that were never truly clear to her. An insurmountable barrier divided her and Julian, aspects of his soul that were beyond her.

At some stage of his report, Julian lost patience and fell silent. Until that moment, Reut had managed to improvise responses that covered up her lack of focus, while Julian nodded mechanically, ostensibly ignoring the disconnect between his words and hers.

"Should I take anything into the living room?" he asked, suddenly frantic. Not waiting for his mother's response, he grabbed the tart and announced, "I'll be right back for the cheese."

Alone in the kitchen, Reut returned to the stove and relit the burner. She fixed her eyes on the coffee that was warming up a second time, letting it imbue her with calm. How Reut loved the sight of the thick foam on top of the Turkish cof-fee and its powerful aroma. The wonderful scent of cooked cardamom. When the coffee was hot enough, Reut placed the pot on a wooden tray, leaned in, and inhaled with plea-sure. This was a ritual she'd repeated for as long as she could remember. She'd adopted it from her father, whom she used to help make coffee every Saturday morning.

When Reut moved to Paris, she'd brought the ritual with her. Jean-Claude appreciated it too, but he was sorry to find that within a few years she neglected the habit. The reason Reut offered: lack of time and necessary energy. The reason she kept to herself: the caffeinated aroma spurred a sense of melancholy and longing for Israel. But what did she have to long for? Every time she visited Israel, she was reminded of how unhappy she used to be there and how she sought relief from its explicit public tension, along with the censorious private tension within her family. Sometimes Reut thought she must just miss her own childhood, that animalistic sense of belonging without judgment that she used to feel within her surroundings.

Reut lingered by the stove for a few moments longer, leaning her elbows against the counter. She had to return to her guests. The coffee was ready. Stefan's ingratiating face appeared before her again. That octopus hand taking hold of her, then resting against her cheek, then her son's pale countenance emerged in her mind . . .

Floating between thoughts, Reut didn't even notice Julian, who'd returned quietly to the kitchen to get the cheese. Nor did she notice Jean-Claude, who'd come to see what the hell was keeping her. Not as stealthy as his son, Jean-Claude didn't hesitate to make his presence known: "Tutu!"

Reut jumped at the sound of his voice, emitting a sound like a door with rusty hinges.

"Ha, ha! Gave you a fright, did I?"

Reut didn't respond. She disliked statements intended only to repeat the obvious.

"Go on, everyone's waiting for you," he said. "What else is there to bring out?"

"Nothing," she said drily. "Go back in, I'll be right there." Then, three seconds later: "No, you know what? Take the, the plate, with, with the patisserie. I'll be right in with the coffee."

As promised, less than a minute later, Reut delivered the coffee tray to the guests. She walked into the living room like an invisible woman, then with slow, measured steps approached and placed the tray on the table. She sat down beside Beatrice, who, barely noticing, offered her a mechanical polite smile and then returned her eyes to Julian, who was sermonizing.

Reut watched her son for a few moments. She tried to listen to him like everyone else, despite having missed the preceding discussion. Then she sprang to her feet, furious with herself for having forgotten to pour the coffee into cups. When the final cup was filled, she sat back down and made another attempt at listening.

"—xample . . . Nevertheless, the film contains some problematic articulation, shall we say, of the tension between his own artistic vision and his constant need to please his audience. And it just doesn't work, this . . . this articulation."

"What do you mean?" Jean-Claude asked, his expression amused. "Please, elaborate, so that we may understand."

Julian shot his father a sour look and fell silent. How he loathed that smile that combined condescension, disdain, and obvious pleasure. Uncomfortably, he tried to keep going, shifting his eyes from Jean-Claude to Stefan. "What I'm trying to say is that I see no connection between this film and

Little Emmanuelle, for instance. Or his masterpiece, *Almighty Men*. It's quite amazing, honestly, that the person who made *Almighty Men* makes such garbage now." He sighed with astonishment, then added, "The tragedy of Berloff is shared by all of us."

"What are you talking about?" Antoine cried. "*Pardon*, but that's—how should I put this? My experience of the movie was entirely different. And another thing: with all due respect to *Almighty Men*, in many ways I believe *The New Regime* surpasses it. *The New Regime* is the smartest, ripest film Berloff has ever made. And I'm the last person who would say—"

"Sure," Julian cut him off. "Everyone says that precisely because everyone says that. Did everyone who says that actually watch the movie? That's a whole other question."

"Julian!" Jean-Claude scolded, but Antoine spoke over him.

Reut's attention wandered again from the conversation to the tea she'd forgotten to offer her guests. She turned her eyes to Beatrice, signaling to her to move her legs and allow her to wriggle out.

She returned from the kitchen carrying the steaming kettle, just in time for Julian's conclusion.

"—it's like this, all the films, the only thing they know how to do today is feed their audience with a spoon. The possibility that people might actually use their brains as they watch a movie is bad for the studios. It would mean a financial flop. People like Berloff, who used to make films such as *Little*

Emmanuelle, can no longer afford to, see? Now they have to justify the enormous budgets they receive for every movie. So they make a new movie every year, but there's nothing new about it. It's always the same three or four talentless stars. They throw away the money on special effects. They spend money on everything except a good screenplay." Julian went quiet, shooting Grigoryev a quick look, intentionally evading his father's gaze, and then, while slicing a handsome chunk of Reblochon, "What I'm actually talking about is—well, it's clearly not"—he took a bite of the cheese—"A good screenplay is exactly what can't work these days. It might break the cycle of stupidity that art is trapped in. And when I say 'cycle of stupidity,' what I mean is the manner in which cinema creates a stupid audience that aspires to watch superficial cinema. Or perhaps the opposite is true. Such a vicious cycle!" He took a moment to consider this, and then, with his eyes still fixed on Antoine, he said, "And obviously I'm not referring to independent cinema, which occasionally produces something more or less worthy."

Berloff was not mentioned again after the discussion of his films concluded. The guests had made sure to erase the controversial name from their consciousness and move on; the evening's success hinged on the suppression of loaded topics. In an instant, all that the guests cared about was the next phase of the dinner party saga—the fabulous flavors of pastries and cheeses, where they had been purchased, the similarities and differences between them, and how they ranked against other pastries and cheeses sampled in the past.

When an excellent slice of Beaufort was polished off, Grigoryev patted his wife's thigh lightly, and said in a refined whisper, "Katyushinka, *davai* . . . let's go."

The important couple stood up right away. Pleasant smiles were offered to everyone who was still seated. Jean-Claude rushed to his feet. Wearing a smug expression, hands in pockets, he walked over and started with Katya's cheeks. Two brief kisses, a warm glance, and then he turned to Grigoryev.

"It was wonderful to have you, Mikhail," he hummed with emotion.

The famous writer kissed both of Jean-Claude's cheeks, and then said, as he shook the man's hand, "The pleasure was all ours."

In spite of the goodbyes, Jean-Claude and Grigoryev remained standing together for a while longer, discussing the practicalities of their next meeting. Jean-Claude wanted to make sure that the *vernissage* they'd discussed was, indeed, scheduled for next Thursday evening. Toward the end of the main course, the idea of inviting Jean-Claude to the exhibition opening formulated in Grigoryev's mind: he thought it would be a fabulous opportunity to introduce the philosopher to Julia Bidot, a close friend and a gifted photographer.

While the two of them talked, Julian sliced himself a small piece of Gruyère, refilled his wineglass, and rushed off to his bedroom with his loot. Reut started clearing the dishes. Physically and mentally exhausted, she didn't even realize that the important guests were leaving, and was hoping that cleaning up would bring the evening to a close. She was glad to find Beatrice and Louise in the kitchen, volunteering to help. Stefan walked in, wearing a morose expression, placed the tea tray on the table, and left.

"How are you getting home?" Reut asked after the second round of dish clearing. She leaned languidly against one of the cabinets.

"We're taking the Metro," Louise replied.

"Ah-*bon*?" Beatrice squeaked. "Maybe we can give you a ride?"

"Oh, *merciiii*," Louise responded on an exhale, as was the Parisian custom. "If you don't mind, that would be *super*!"

A moment's thought.

"No, come to think of it, there's no need. You live by Saint-Georges? No, no, it would be too out of the way for you. Really there's no need."

"Don't be silly!" Beatrice insisted. "Just let me check with Antoine . . ."

After the friendly exchange, the trio returned to the living room. Beatrice walked over to Antoine while Reut and Louise pulled out their cellphones. Then, seated on the sofa, each woman enjoyed a private moment with her device, checking for any new messages. Then, out of mindless habit, they both perused their apps and news sites, checking if anything new and interesting had been posted. To their disappointment, no worthy item or update attracted their attention. This frustration prompted a repeated, more thorough perusal of their feeds. Louise found one superficial item of note, if only for the spasm of laughter it sent rolling through her.

Reut scooted closer to Louise to read the amusing post. But before she had a chance to ask her friend what was so funny, Beatrice's meek voice announced, "We can do it! We'll give you a ride."

"Oh, *fantastique!*" Louise cried, her face still illuminated by the hilarious online feed.

Rising from the sofa, Reut dreamily scanned the room for a few moments until, all of a sudden, she heard Antoine's commanding voice.

"All right, *allez*, let's go!"

At the sound of his order, Beatrice walked over to her husband, who was already standing by the door with Stefan and Jean-Claude. Tossing her hair, she turned her back on Antoine, her smile hinting at him to help her with her coat.

Louise also joined them at the door. Sighing with satisfaction, she summed up the evening: "It was lovely."

"It really was wonderful!" Beatrice confirmed.

"Thanks for coming!" Jean-Claude cheered.

"Thanks for having us," said Stefan.

"And the food," Antoine added, "excellent as usual!"

These words of gratitude were prelude to the "*Au revoir*, kiss-kiss," ritual that Jean-Claude conducted with the guests. It took a moment for Reut to realize the ceremony had commenced, and she joined the pecking exchange as well. Beatrice's right cheek, left cheek, fabulous. Onward to Stefan's right cheek, left cheek, wonderful! That awkward moment they'd shared was buried deep in her subconscious. But then, as her body turned toward Antoine—an instinctive paralysis, a sudden urge for fresh air that rendered her participation in the kissing ritual redundant.

"Where did you park?" she asked.

"We circled the place a few times," Antoine murmured. "We ended up parking a few blocks away."

She debated the point for a moment, then said, "I'll walk you to your car."

"But it really is quite far—"

"I'm coming with you."

The group walked out of the building quietly. It was very cold outside, so different from that morning, when the winter sun had balanced out the cold wind. Now, under the moon's light, all Reut could feel was a petrifying cold. Startled by the gust of wind, she removed her scarf and rewrapped it to cover her lips as well. How she hated the European weather! From the moment winter began (winter by her definition; autumn according to Europeans), every time she set out from home amounted to nothing short of a military operation: her only wish was to reach her destination as quickly as possible.

But that Friday night was different. There was no particular reason for her to go outside, no place where people were waiting for her. All Reut knew, or, rather, felt, was that she had to get some air, to walk, to give priority to bodily sensation over cerebral thought. She didn't want to speak. She wanted no more small talk. The guests served as her excuse to step outside, but all she yearned for was to be left alone. Unfortunately, the two couples beside her seemed to be enjoying the nocturnal jaunt. At some point, somebody even declared the weather "lovely!"

Reut walked on in silence, matching her pace to the group's. One of her hands was tucked in her coat pocket, while the other held the scarf against her face. She breathed heavily into the fleece, feeling her body heat intensify. Focused on her own footsteps, she didn't notice when Antoine came to a surprise stop, forcing the entire group to halt.

"Is something wrong?" Louise inquired.

"I'm not—just a moment . . ." Antoine mumbled, looking around, unblinking. A few seconds later, as he spun around, Antoine said, "One moment, didn't I park here? It's—"

"*Oh la la*!" Beatrice roared. "Don't tell me you don't remember where you parked!"

"Just a second, just be quiet for a second . . ." Antoine fell silent, trying to keep his cool.

The group seemed utterly despondent. One was already contemplating calling a cab, another was convinced that the car had been towed. But then—surprise! Without a word, Antoine broke into a fast, auspicious strut. The others followed the diminishing figure of their would-be driver, sharing glimmers of hope that he was on track. Even Reut put on an excited expression, though her heart foretold disappointment.

"*Alors*?" Beatrice asked hopefully.

"Nothing!"

"My goodness," she cried in distress.

A few moments of silence. Nobody knew quite what to do or say. Reut held back from announcing she was going home. But while her mind began to stray, the impossible happened—Antoine's repressed memory erupted from his unconscious as quickly and powerfully as boiling magma!

"*Bah-oui!*" he cried, breaking into a run, then he signaled from a distance: there was the car!

Reut said goodbye to the guests, concluding the parting ceremony. When she was far enough away, she sighed loudly. A few steps later, she sighed again, softer this time, longing to be alone. Without thinking about her route, a canine sense carried her legs in the direction of home. And yet, a third of the way back, she paused and turned around. It wasn't yet her bedtime. Her legs begged for more motion, more speed, more time in the Parisian night.

"*Nifla*, wonderful," she mumbled in Hebrew, smiling. Then, in French, while quickening her footsteps: "*C'est bien. Très bien . . .*"

In spite of Reut's ingrained hatred of winter, almost nothing pleased her more than the moment when her body warmed up so much that she felt the need to remove her layers—first gloves, then scarf and coat—and her pleasure was intensified if she could do this on an empty street. Then she gave herself over to the movement, propelling her awakening, burning body, driven by some invisible force that almost urged her to break into a run, to forget her high-heeled boots and forsake all thoughts and worries—until the moment she was forced to stop.

She was out of breath.

By the corner pharmacy, Reut paused, panting with satisfaction, at this late hour that marked the end of Friday. After staring at the green neon signage for a few seconds, waiting for her heart to stop pounding, she continued wandering the desolate neighborhood, this time with fatigue. A cold wave overtook her, and she grumbled for having removed her warm layers, and rushed to put them back on. It was time to go home.

Eagerly punching in the building's entry code, Reut pushed the front door open with her shoulder. She felt exhausted and utterly impatient. Everything had become unbearable. Before she called the elevator, she waged battle with the scarf, which was suffocating her like a python. So hot. Why would this god-awful piece of fabric not relent?! So terribly hot. Oh, good, success! She shoved the scarf into her purse, went upstairs, and busied herself. First, she removed her coat and hung it in the foyer, then pulled off the sweater she'd slipped on over her dress, and finally wriggled out of her boots, freeing her feet from their leather prison. In the kitchen, she poured herself some cold water and gulped it down. She poured a second glass, took a few slower sips, and poured the rest down the drain. Then, in the bathroom, she cleaned her face. No matter the circumstances, Reut almost never skipped this step. Too many times, she'd heard tales of dangers lurking for women who slept in their makeup.

After a perfunctory wash, Reut still had a few more things to do—and then they all faded away. Only a single task remained in her mind: removing her dress and tight pantyhose before slipping into bed. Much like the scarf, these items also put up a fight. Finally, in nothing but her under-wear, she stood at the closet, randomly pulling out a white T-shirt and slipping it on. She glanced at the bed, noticing Jean-Claude for the first time since entering the room. He was lying on his back, mouth half-open, arm tossed over his head. She dove into the empty spot beside him, placed an embracing arm around his chest, and was pulled into a sleep that, the next morning, would seem as barren as a desert.

PART II

A TRIP

TARTINE

REUT was fully awake by 7:18 a.m. It was eight minutes after her alarm clock rang the first time, and three minutes after it went off the second time. She didn't think she'd need that second backup alarm, not on the busy day she had been looking forward to. A day of travel! As soon as she saw the time, stress took over. She jumped out of bed while chastising herself, persisting with the rebukes all the way to the bathroom, and stopping only when the water hit her naked body.

In an instant, her legs petrified, followed by the rest of her limbs. She stood under the stream immobilized and free of thoughts. As she quickly walked back to the bedroom, she realized she had no idea how long she'd spent in the shower. Stress had the upper hand. But it was only 7:36; she'd have no problem completing all of her morning tasks before leaving.

It was a Tuesday in August, and a joyously sunny morning. Sunlight streamed softly into the kitchen, putting an end to the capricious grayness that had painted over Paris for the past five days; an immutable grayness falling upon residents and tourists, who bemoaned global warming yet celebrated every warm, sunny day. Sometimes, Reut wondered how the blue Paris sky still managed to excite her. She had detested the sun as a child, searching for shade wherever she went. Even as an adult, each summertime visit to Israel felt vexed. Analyzing this disconnect between her love of sunshine in Paris and her hatred of the Israeli sun, Reut concluded that it wasn't the thing itself that affected her mood, but the surprising departure from habit. And nothing could make Reut happier that morning than pervasive sunshine.

Already dressed and wearing makeup, standing silently by the kitchen window, Reut indulged for several moments in that entrancing view: a street bathed in light, still devoid of people, sunrays announcing a vacation. *It'll be good, it'll do you good*, she told herself softly. Then she made sure to close the window properly, and checked the other windows around the apartment. When she finished this inspection, she paced her home frantically, making sure one last time that everything was in its place, locked and turned off. After that, she dragged her suitcase to the front door and reviewed her final list: Passport? Plane ticket? Check. Wallet? Check. Phone charger? She wasn't sure. She rummaged through her bag. Check. Excellent. She left the apartment. She still had work to do.

Reut examined her reflection in the brasserie's glass entryway and rubbed at a smudge of concealer. She lumbered inside slowly, pushing open the heavy door while carrying her suitcase and handbag.

Leisurely removing her shawl, she looked around for an

open table, then jumped with a start at the sound of a greeting addressed at her. It was Mathieu, a waiter with over twenty years of experience at the brasserie, and Reut's favorite.

"Madame," he said in his deep tenor.

He led her to a table and asked if she'd like to sit there.

No, absolutely not, she determined, shaking her head. The table was too close to the early birds chatting at the bar, and today she could not afford to be distracted: there was a British thriller she'd been commissioned to translate, which she'd put off to the last minute. The result? Three hours before heading to the airport, she still had to translate the final pages!

Reut hated to be rushed. She didn't perform well under pressure, was not the type who, at the eleventh hour, found within themselves a well of hidden power. She typically worked slowly, carefully, always aspiring to complete the work before the agreed-upon deadline. What happened to her with this book? With the other books she'd taken on over the past year? Reut could not give an answer to this question, neither to herself nor to the Israeli publisher. With each new book placed in her care, she grew more restless and her ability to concentrate diminished.

As the deadline for the British thriller approached, she knew there was no choice but to speak to Jean-Claude. She informed him that she had to postpone her flight to Puglia in order to finish the work. It would be only a three-day delay. "An imperceptible delay," according to her; "a baffling, aggravating delay," according to him.

News of what her husband referred to as "the important vacation" had reached Reut two months earlier. She remembered the night of the announcement well: she'd thrown out her back and was struggling to progress in her work on an erotic novel, which she'd been translating alongside the British book. Jean-Claude, as usual, was oblivious to anyone other than himself.

He came home around 11:30 at night, slammed the front door behind him, and, his expression self-satisfied and his breath smelling of wine, called out, "Tutu, *chérie!*"

"What?" she groaned, turning her wilted back slightly.

"I've got news for you. This summer"—four steps toward her desk—"this summer, we're going to take a very special vacation."

"Ah-*oui*?" she mumbled, returning her eyes to the screen.

A few moments went by while Jean-Claude spoke and Reut didn't listen. Her entire being was focused on her effort to translate the English prose. She often thought that Jean-Claude seemed to derive unique pleasure from interrupting her at work. But when it came to his own work? The morning hours, which he spent answering emails, were circled with a halo of sanctity: she must never get in his way.

"Well," he began, sitting down beside her, "at the end of August we'll be going to his house in southern Italy. Don't worry, *chérie*, I'll have exact dates later this week. He's supposed to tell me in the next few days."

"What? Who?"

"Mikhail."

Reut nodded. Her eyes wandered from the computer to the bound pages she'd been laboring to translate. There were quite a few intriguing passages, but she wasn't satisfied with the way she'd translated them.

"Tutu," Jean-Claude protested, "why don't you cut it out with the—"

"With what?"

"With the . . . " He paused for three seconds. "*Putain*! I'm trying to tell you something!"

Reut pulled her eyes away from the screen to meet Jean-Claude's withering gaze. After a brief staring contest, she surrendered: in spite of her shot nerves, her husband's childish desire to share something with her was enough to soften her heart and inspire her to ask for more details. Jean-Claude happily obliged and recounted his meeting with Grigoryev, the fifth so far, which had ended on an extremely positive note. He finally arrived at the key point: "A few years ago, he bought a summer home in Puglia, in southern Italy, you know, near Naples . . . " A moment's pause, then, to himself: "He's absolutely right. Tuscany has become impossible. The tourists had completely ruined it! It's—" Addressing Reut again: "I can't believe we haven't gone there yet! I—oh, yes, there was that time, that summer we wanted to join Marco and Federica, right, Tutu? I can't remember why we didn't go. At any rate, it's going to be wonderful! I've been wanting to see the cathedral there for a long time. And anyway, Mikhail told me that the entire area is gorgeous. Very special. Lots of different places to see."

"Good."

"And the house," Jean-Claude continued, "the house is in a small town called . . . one moment . . . Polignano a Mare. A beautiful place. He's going to spend August there with Katya and his brother and another couple, and asked if we wanted to join. I said of course. I knew you'd be thrilled!"

Reut confirmed her husband's assumption, even though she hadn't yet herself decided how she felt about the vacation. It was only the next morning that she began processing the information, swinging like a pendulum between opinions on the subject. But on the night of the announcement, Reut was in no state to seriously consider the trip. Her mind was pre-occupied with the erotic novel, which she found mediocre, and with her injured back. And so she asked to continue the conversation the following day and encouraged Jean-Claude to go to bed. He half listened to her, focused on his fingers fluttering over her long neck, stretching into a caress. Her skin was warm and soft, he noticed.

This discovery lifted him off the chair, and he placed his lips on Reut's neck to feel that thrilling warmth and soft-ness all the more intensely. They were small butterfly kisses at first, searching kisses, alternated by nibbles of her earlobe. Eyes closed, Reut mumbled some words of rejection, plac-ing her hands against Jean-Claude's chest in the gesture of a shove (though, in fact, they were too limp to shove anything at all). Jean-Claude's lips continued wandering, running up and down her neck, inviting his tongue to join in. All of a sudden, impatient, they clung to Reut's lips. Then, with renewed self-restraint, he gave her slow, playful kisses, alternately fluttering and aggressive. At the same time, his hand got acquainted with Reut's inner thigh, moving in circular, sensual motions from her crotch, then back to her thighs, then crotch again.

Jean-Claude was certainly in high spirits that night. His unusual patience, his friskiness. Reut hadn't expected that! His touch was pleasant, especially after spending the day translating erotica (in spite of the bad writing, the novel had awakened her body, heightening her sensitivity without her even noticing). Gradually, she began to surrender to her husband, less preoccupied with outside distractions and more attuned to her body and the profound sensations awakening within it.

Then, all of a sudden: renewed awareness, remembering the goals she'd set. Jean-Claude kept touching her, never ceasing, at times rubbing too hard. She tried to tell him to stop, but it took a few moments for the command to leave her mouth. She still wasn't sure what she wanted . . . Finally, softly, she said, "Hmm . . . stop . . ." Eyes still partly closed, she grabbed Jean-Claude's hand and pulled it off her crotch.

Jean-Claude, all aglow, interpreted her instruction as a request for variety.

Variety? No problem! In a second, her bra was unhooked and tossed to the floor, his wide palms burrowing into her breasts. A few more moments went by, Jean-Claude moaning, his lips exploring her left breast, and then Reut repeated, "Stop."

A few seconds later: "Later, *chéri*. I have to finish this . . . "

"*Bien sûr*," he replied, replacing his hand aggressively on her crotch, inflamed by her refusal.

A few more seconds of inhibited pleasure, then, more sternly: "Enough. This is not a good time."

Reut stood up quickly and took a few steps away.

Now a protective abyss lay between them.

It took Reut several minutes to regain her concentration after Jean-Claude left the kitchen. It was getting late, but she forbade herself from getting up from her seat until she finished translating the penultimate chapter. She didn't want to keep putting things off and was not yet ready to join Jean-Claude in bed. Enforcing self-discipline, she remained in her seat for two hours longer, ignoring her screaming bladder, which begged for a break. When her mission was accomplished, she had trouble getting up. The neglected bladder punished her with intense pain.

Having limped to the bathroom, Reut plopped onto the toilet and closed her eyes. A strong, yellow stream shot out of her, furious and out of control. When it finally stopped, Reut remained on the toilet for several more minutes, utterly exhausted. Then, forgetting her face cleansing ritual, she made her way to the bedroom where she crawled into bed to find that Jean-Claude could sense her presence from within his sleep and still desired her. His dreams were surely emblazoned with images of an Italian getaway as his body yearned for climax.

Passively, she submitted to him.

From the night of the announcement to the day of the trip, Reut had submitted to Jean-Claude's sexual urges quite a few times. His strengthening bond with Grigoryev and the shared vacation on the horizon imbued him with a powerful *joie de vivre*. But Reut couldn't share his excitement. In the two months prior to the flight, she mostly felt exhaustion and stress. The translation work, the doctoral dissertation—they all seemed bungled and beyond her abilities. Reut struggled with that same self-doubt at the brasserie on the morning of the Puglia journey, skeptical she'd manage to complete her translation in the three hours she had at her disposal.

She thought she'd tracked down a table isolated enough to serve her professional purposes. "I'd love to sit there, if possible," she said to Mathieu, pointing at the left corner of the brasserie, at a small table by the window.

"*Bien sûr*, madame," Mathieu said. After finally seating her, he asked her if she wanted her "coffee as usual."

"Of course," she replied, adding that this morning she'd be ordering some food, too. After debating what kind of carbohydrates she desired, she chose the item she almost always wanted to order and almost always decided to forego: the tartine!

In spite of Reut's fondness for tartine, she only rarely allowed herself to indulge in it, both because of the excess calories, and because of the time and tranquility it demanded. The brasserie's tartine was exceptionally delectable: served with fabulous organic Normandy butter and artisanal blueberry jam, prepared by a celebrated Parisian *pâtissier*.

After ordering, she couldn't help but notice the small wrinkles of surprise on Mathieu's forehead. As he walked away, far enough to justify raising her voice: "And, if you can, make the coffee really boiling. You know how I like it . . ."

As she awaited her tartine and piping hot coffee, Reut extricated the British thriller and laptop from her bag and placed them on the table ceremoniously. She shifted the laptop a little to the right, then a little to the left, pushing it as far away from her as the table allowed, then pulling it a few inches closer. Pleased with the setup, Reut opened the novel at the bookmark and glanced at the page. From there, her eyes wandered dreamily toward the window, which offered a view of the street where the hubbub was speeding up. Right to left, left to right, lonely people, sometimes couples, or trios at most, all walked past the wide window, making their way toward one destination or another. Some walked briskly, others with an unhurried ease that irritated Reut. She watched them, all those strangers she thought she knew, whose essence she could see. Faces emerging and disappearing before her eyes as if in a moving train, cheerful faces, self-satisfied. It had to be the warm sun that was responsible for their uplifted spirits: excitement for their upcoming vacations, sublime expectations.

And why shouldn't they be thrilled to take a break? They must have felt entitled to it. They'd earned it thanks to their industriousness and patience. Some had already decided on their special holiday: a conquest of the unknown, an encounter with a new place; or a return to a favorite destination, a self-appropriated bit of geography. Even if Reut belonged to the former group—the intrepid explorers group—that morning she lacked the wherewithal to feel appropriately excited. Gloomy premonitions of boredom among the Grigoryev tribe wrangled with fantasies of nighttime piazzas and Italian banquets.

"*Voilà!*" Mathieu announced, appearing with a tray of delicacies.

Reut jumped up, tearing her eyes away from the window, and was gripped by helplessness. She should have known the table would be too small. Coyly, she asked Mathieu if switching tables would be an issue. Two tables down, she spotted a larger one that would be ideal.

Mathieu paused, engaging in a series of silent calculations. Then, with a mixture of reproach and mischief, he offered, "Madame, only for you. Allow me."

Once the transfer of her belongings had been completed, Reut sat down somewhat stiffly on the wooden chair and adjusted her laptop's placement again.

She opened the book. A few moments of mindless staring as her hand found the coffee cup. A careful sip. The coffee had already cooled. Her eyes shifted over to the translation file on the screen. Another sip, a frustrated exhale. Then, in Hebrew, "*Kadima, nu*, let's go already."

She read the final sentence she'd translated. Fine. Just fine. She pushed her chair closer to the table and sat up straight. Five minutes of work, and then: "Ah! What's wrong with me . . ." She turned sharply toward her bag and pulled out her cellphone.

No missed calls.

The work went on. She advanced through a page and a half. Fantastic! She couldn't help herself and checked her phone again. Indeed, as she'd assumed: still nothing. It was almost 9:15. Reut was gripped by panic, coupled with a violent hunger. She hadn't yet found a chance to eat her tartine. Reut pushed the book away and pulled the baguette closer. She ripped off a respectable hunk with gusto, then pounced upon the butter and extracted an ample lump with her knife. She started smearing the bread with clumsy, impatient motions, working to coat the surface equally.

In the middle of her next bite, Reut pushed the food away. Hand on her chest, she attended to the intense pounding of her heart. Focused on her breathing, she closed her eyes and tried to soothe herself. She took a distracted sip of coffee, then stared for several minutes at an empty seat in front of her. Once her breath was almost back to normal, she glanced around to make sure no one had been watching. Most of the café goers seemed lost in conversation.

Reut silenced her phone and tossed it back into her bag. She spent the next long hour focused on the words before her. Surprising herself, she made it to the book's final page. One last effort. Rewarding herself with a brief break, she closed the screen and looked around, noting that the crowd had changed. Couples, families. People who liked an early lunch. The table closest to hers was swarmed by a small family dining together. Reut hadn't even noticed them before. Enough! She wasn't finished yet, she couldn't afford to lose concentration now. She quickly opened the screen, exhaled loudly, and turned to the final page.

Attempting to read the first line, Reut's finger strayed to the plate, hunted down a scrumptious crumb, and inserted it into her mouth. She did this with a few more crumbs, her eyes fixed on the page.

"*Pfff*," she huffed. "Enough already."

Her scolding did nothing to help the situation. In an instant, she left her seat and rushed to the bathroom, hoping not to attract anyone's attention, or worse—conversation. She walked right into the stall, her eyes skipping the mirror. She was too afraid to look at her reflection, nor did she have the time: the familiar stabbing sensation was back. She felt an intense urge to sit down and close her eyes for a few moments. But this required some preparation. Nothing came easily to her. Without wasting a moment, she ripped a few strips of toilet paper and placed them on the toilet seat one at a time, careful not to leave any exposed space. She was nearly finished when, like a game of Jenga, the entire construction collapsed into the toilet.

To start all over again.

How to start all over?

Reut had neither the motivation nor the strength to do that. She squatted instead, hovering over the toilet. When she finished relieving herself, she lingered in the stall a little longer, taking advantage of this rare moment of solitude to stretch out her aching limbs. She hoped to unlock the tight vertebrae of her back, which suffered from the prolonged time spent sitting. When she left the bathroom, her mood was much improved.

She had a little less than half an hour to complete the translation. Not much time, but it might be enough. With a tense wave of the hand, she signaled to one of the waiters for an espresso. In the meantime, she fished out her wallet to settle the bill, then downed the espresso in a single gulp before diving back into the text.

Reut finished translating the book into Hebrew within twenty minutes and then focused her eyes on the screen for a while, taking in her achievement. One more book. One more goal attained. Reut was perpetually aware of the challenge of translation. But now, unlike Reut the doctoral student, who saw translation as much more than a means of making a living, the Reut sitting in the brasserie felt neither excitement nor pride in her work.

At this stage in life, Reut treated translation as nothing more than a job. A privileged one, she always made sure to remind herself. She was glad to have a profession she didn't loath, and even aspired to excel at. Each book gave birth to new ideas and heroes. They passed through her and came to exist independently in other people's minds. And yet, translation for her lacked hidden dreams or secret wishes.

But Reut wanted to feel elated about it. She wanted to be asked what she did for a living and reply "I'm a translator" with the same enthusiasm that anyone who heard the response always exhibited. Each cry of impassioned marvel from a stranger inspired a wave of guilt in her. Why was she unable to feel the satisfaction people expected of her?

Earlier, two years before Reut's Italian getaway, Professor Emeritus Jeffrey Sanderson's death had awakened other suppressed aspirations. She traveled to California to attend his funeral, joining conversations with other mourners that shed light on his genius and modesty, a dying breed. As soon as she landed back in Paris, she made up her mind to reenroll in a PhD program, aware of the two central challenges this decision involved: first, she had to stop persistently criticizing herself, and second, she had to summon the courage to endure Jean-Claude's reaction. As she expected, he took the news coldly, focusing on the difficulties her choice would entail.

TAXI

REUT had no trouble finding the taxi she'd called. The driver was across the street, leaning against the car door, stretching out his neck as he puffed on a cigarette. He seemed to know how to enjoy a brief wait in the sunshine.

"*Bonjour*," she called, waving to him.

"*Bonjour!*" he replied with earnest cheerfulness, flashing her a grin.

He pursed his lips around the cigarette, took the suitcase from Reut, and slipped it into the trunk. She slid into the back seat, pleasantly surprised by the intoxicating aroma of leather.

Once he took his seat behind the wheel and slammed the door, the driver said, "To the airport then?"

"Yes, Charles de Gaulle, please."

A brief pause.

"It shouldn't take more than thirty minutes to get there, right? I have a flight to catch."

"What's that, mademoiselle?" the driver cried gleefully, turning his head so she wouldn't miss his wide smile. "So where are you traveling to?"

A three-second silence.

"Italy."

"Italy!" he echoed. "Good. But—" the driver fell silent, navigating a tricky crosswalk, then continued, "Where is your accent from?"

"Pardon?"

"Where's the sweet accent from?" Then, without waiting for an answer, the driver embarked on a little game.

"*Buongiorno!*"

Silence.

"No," he carried on. "Not Italian . . . Spain, then!"

"No . . ."

Early in the game, Reut considered whether she should just reveal the answer so that he would leave her alone. Experience had taught her that sharing her home country with strangers could inspire one of two extreme, equally aggravating responses: excessive excitement or disappointment and distaste.

After three more wrong guesses, Reut finally broke down and told him.

"From Israel?" he bellowed, placing himself, to her surprise, in the excessively excited camp. "*Walla, ya habibti!*" he exclaimed in Arabic, then switched back to French, "*Bien sûr, bien sûr!* And what is the lovely lady's name?"

"Pardon?"

"Can't hear compliments? I asked what is the lovely lady's name!"

"Oh," she murmured. "Reut."

"Ut?" he asked.

"Re-ut. Yes, it's a difficult name . . ."

"Reut. *Walla* . . . pretty name. *Enchanté*, Reut."

Reut offered a reserved smile. "And you?"

"I'm Ahmed. You know, Re-ut," Ahmed's voice suddenly rose, in a performative fashion, "my cousin's friend, a good friend of his, recently visited Israel. He told me he went to, to Tel Aviv, and to, *walla*, some other town. What was the name of it? Yes—the one with the salty sea. He loved it there. Parties all day long, he told me! Beautiful women!" Ahmed clicked his tongue, sighed, and said, "You know, mademoiselle, I . . . I have many Jewish friends. Many Jewish customers. Very good people. Truly." He nodded and smiled at Reut, silent for a brief spell. "What, and, tell me . . ." Ahmed mumbled, opening the window. "And what d—thi—ab—yo—pri—ter?"

"Pardon?" Reut shouted over the roaring of the wind, shifting a lock of hair that had flown into her eyes.

"What—think—your—ime minister?" he repeated.

Overcome by sudden distress, Reut yelled rudely that she couldn't really talk with the window open on the highway. The driver immediately rolled up the window and repeated his question a third time.

I wish he hadn't done that, she thought.

"Um . . . I don't know, I don't know if I'm the right person to ask about politics."

"*Walla.*"

Reut used the brief silence to look out the window and unwind, but Ahmed again insisted on bringing up the all too familiar topic. "But there's always a war going on there, no?

I—just so you know—I . . . I have nothing against the Jews. Certainly not. But your politicians, I do . . . I definitely have a problem with them! Dangerous people. Listen to me. But Jews? No way! I told you, mademoiselle, I have many Jewish friends. Lots, lots of customers. Nothing but war all day long, huh?! Everywhere that . . . and by the way, that's exactly why I came here, you see? You know how long I've been here? It's been—wait . . ."

He calculated.

"*Walla*, seventeen years. Can you imagine? I've been here seventeen years already! That's—" Ahmed fell silent, taking a moment with his thoughts. "You want to know why I left my country? Listen, I'll tell you why I left. I want peace and quiet, you understand? I'd had enough. Because, because I want to live. I want a life for my family."

"*D'accord*," Reut said. There was a question on the tip of her tongue that she held back when Ahmed exploded all of a sudden at a brash driver.

"Son of a whore!" he yelled, surrendering to his rage. "Did you see him?! Did you see how that maniac cut me off?!" Rather boldly, Ahmed started clapping his hands as he continued to fly down the highway: "Bravo! Son of a bitch . . ."

Once he'd calmed down, Reut asked, "So did you find your peace and quiet here?"

"What?!"

"I asked if, if you found peace and quiet here, here in Paris."

Ahmed seemed confused, as if this were a trick question. He prattled on, the edges of his lips pulling downward like a fishhook. Finally, he said, "*Walla*, things aren't so simple here, either."

Like a flood, the end of which she could not predict, Ahmed's explanation washed over Reut. For more than ten minutes, the taxi driver listed the reasons that his life and his family's life were so challenging. Reut listened at first, her face wearing an expression of empathy as she nodded, interjecting an occasional decorous *d'accord* to prove attentiveness. She truly did pay attention for the first two or three minutes. It wasn't easy to hear the revealing information Ahmed was sharing, and she was saddened to learn about the unfair course of his life.

And yet, she soon lost focus. Like a dancer fumbling through her choreography without a mirror, Reut faltered through the taxi ride, continuing to nod, appallingly out of step with Ahmed's words. She felt guilty once she realized this, but couldn't refocus. Her head was too full of thoughts, she told herself. Chock-full. Her clogged mind worked overtime, scampering about against the backdrop of Ahmed's voice. Most central was a problem that had popped up only a week earlier, and had remained dormant until now, when that minor memory floated to the surface and took on a new form. The physical effects were immediate: a quickened heartbeat and an obsessive twirling of her hair.

It had been nothing more than an anecdote, the kind pulled out to entertain on boring evenings. And the entertainer that night had been Shira, who called Reut for no particular reason.

"So, how do you feel about the big trip?" Shira asked, to justify her call.

"Fine," Reut said, then interrogated Shira about her use of the word "big." She asked Shira defiantly if she wanted to join them so that she, too, could enjoy the venerable company of the "big writer." Baffled at the attack, Shira found herself at a critical junction with only two potential paths: defensiveness or contrition. Though she didn't believe the latter was called for and found no logic whatsoever in Reut's onslaught, she opted for an apology, claiming she'd misspoken.

Suspicious, Reut let the small talk run on. With the phone against her ear, she wandered from the living room into the kitchen, listening to Shira's monologue. Reut found her friend's chattiness soothing for a change. All day long she had been exhausting herself with the thriller translation, and now Shira's voice was as mind-numbing as a sitcom episode. But Reut was far from relaxing completely: when she entered the kitchen, she was both surprised and unsurprised to find a pile of begrimed dishes, which led her to open the dishwasher to load it up. But there she found yet another frustrating scene: the dishwasher was full of clean plates that first had to be put away.

As she put the kitchen back in order, her mind drifted away from Shira, until hearing, "You're not going to believe what she told me, this Naomi. You know a woman named Aliza Shor, you two went to Columbia together, right?"

"Yes, we went to grad school together. Why?"

"You aren't going to believe what book, or, rather, *whose* book, Naomi recommended to me."

"I don't know," Reut said. "Aliza's?"

"Yes!" Shira broke into laughter. "How did you know? Did you already hear about it?"

"No, I haven't heard about it. I assumed that's what you meant, Shira."

"Oh! Well, then ... good! Anyway, I couldn't believe I even remembered her name. You haven't mentioned her in years. Didn't the two of you used to be friends back in New York? Well, it turns out that Naomi is very up to date on everything that happens abroad. You know, the literary scene. And what did she tell me?"

Reut closed her eyes with agony, longing for Shira to finish her story already.

"Well, it turns out that Aliza's new book made it onto the *New York Times* bestseller list the week it came out! And apparently it was well deserved. Naomi read the book in just two nights. She said it's chilling. That Aliza has an extraordinary way of looking at life."

"Uh-huh. Goo—" Reut yawned, then sat down on a kitchen chair. "Good."

Reut allowed Shira to go on for another minute, uninterrupted. She felt disconnected, too tired to cut the conversation short and go to bed. But just as she was preparing to bid Shira a good night, Aliza reemerged in her consciousness, and words just spilled out, all of them tinged with suspicion. "So what's the novel even about? Did she say?"

"Oh, Aliza's? Oh, well, honestly I'm not even sure you could call it that. It's a memoir, actually. Naomi told me that Aliza wrote all about her complicated relationship with her mother. The whole book is written in letter form. Oh! I forgot to tell you, you're going to love this! Naomi said that the critics are calling Aliza the female Kafka."

"What? Why?"

"Come on! Because instead of *Letter to His Father*, it's *Letter to Her Mother*! A brilliant idea, isn't it?"

"Uh-huh," Reut said indistinctly, her gaze floating through space, her finger and thumb coming together to peel a bit of dry skin off her lips. After a pause, she said, "Okay, Shira, I must get some rest."

Less than fifteen minutes after hanging up, she was passed out in her bed without finishing most of the tasks she'd planned. Among those she'd neglected were translating an additional page, taking a shower, and electronically tracking the men in her life—making sure Julian was having fun and taking care of himself on his holiday in Portugal, and checking on Jean-Claude's whereabouts.

The next morning, when Reut woke up without an alarm clock at a little after six, she dove into an ocean of work and didn't think of Aliza again. But now, in the taxi, somewhere on the A1 autoroute, all she could think about, all she simply had to think about, was Aliza Shor and her chilling book! Reut was especially preoccupied by the label "the female Kafka," words she repeated in her mind over and over again, each iteration accompanied by the same eye roll and suspicious raised brow. She had no doubt that this was an exaggerated, not to mention ridiculous, comparison, in light of the faded memory she had of Aliza from their school-days. Where did that glowing talent and insight come from? And when did Aliza's relationship with her mother become so complicated? Reut recalled nothing out of the ordinary between Aliza, the good little Jewish American girl, the diligent student, and her mother, wizard of Friday night dinners and hostess extraordinaire. "A memoir"... "Kafka"... "brilliant!" Words that could drive her insane!

At some point in Ahmed's speech, Reut could no longer disguise her turmoil. It was precisely the moment when he started telling her about his distant cousin, whom the Turkish government had imprisoned for no reason, that Reut blurted out, "Ah! What's with this traffic?!"

Without waiting for a response, Reut pulled out her phone and checked the time. Ah! Of course this would happen!

"Everything all right, mademoiselle?" Ahmed stammered, looking at his customer through the rearview mirror. "What, did you lose something?"

"Pardon?" she barked. Then, in Hebrew, "*Hineh zeh.* Here it is! Oh, well."

A brief silence, then Ahmed, having deciphered the cause of her distress, added, "Don't worry. We'll be there in five minutes, Re-ut."

An odd sensation took hold of Reut: she'd almost forgotten she'd given him her first name. Without answering, she shot the back of his neck a sour look, then turned it on the cars stuck in traffic, then at her phone. She repeated this cycle as her mind invented potential scenarios that would unfold if she missed her flight.

Then Ahmed, an eternal optimist, said, "We'll be there in a moment, mademoiselle. Trust me, as soon as this bottleneck breaks up, we'll be at the airport!" He attempted to catch Reut's eyes in the mirror to show her his amused face, to make her laugh. It was a worthy goal that failed miserably: not the faintest smile emerged. Reut's hollow eyes caught his attempts to cheer her up. She wanted to smile, to let go of the tension that petrified her face. But her lips seemed to have been sewed shut, and she was utterly incapable of opening her mouth. And why was that? The voice of reason in her head told her that everything would work out. Everything always did. She'd make her flight. The voice also added that it was her fault for always choosing to indulge in needless stress, falling prey to her own nerves, which were already prone to getting the better of her. And indeed, a brief glance at the idling cars was enough to completely distort her perception of time and space: each minute seemed to last forever, foreboding tragedy.

Traffic let up four minutes later, and Ahmed floored the gas pedal.

"*Bien*," she murmured, still rattled. "Should we listen to the radio?"

But as soon as Ahmed turned it on, Reut regretted her request. The volume was too loud, the song too upbeat. She asked him to change the station, preferably to classical music. Ahmed acquiesced instantly, the smile never leaving his face.

Ravel, *Gaspard de la Nuit.*

Reut recognized it right away. She would know this piece from any movement. She'd first heard it in New York, and the music had a special place in her heart ever since, not necessarily because of the lovely melody, but because of the memory of the moment. It was at Jean-Claude's apartment, just six months after they'd started seeing each other—long enough to feel that she already knew him, that she could be herself around him, but early enough to still be discovering things about him, and to want to impress him. An ongoing dance of distance and proximity. She experienced each intimate moment with intensity, like a window into a possible future, into a potential life she could choose. It was that night when they first listened to Ravel together, two bodies as one, crammed into the small armchair, that Reut knew: this was the future. And, simultaneously: this was the present she must remember, the sweet foundation of their relationship that, one day, she would hold on to.

Ravel's piano notes had the power to instantly assuage her nerves. Leaning heavily against the headrest, she half closed her eyes, not thinking much of anything at all.

Then came the declaration she'd been waiting for: "We're here!"

Her calm dissipated: she had to double-check that everything was ready. In a flash, she adopted the poise of a marathon runner at the start of a race.

After killing the engine, Ahmed opened the door for her with enthusiasm, then nearly ran to the trunk to pull out her suitcase. Before he had a chance to help her out of the car, he found her facing him on the sidewalk.

"*Voilà!*" he proclaimed. "See? No need to worry." Handing over the suitcase, he cheered her on: "Quick!"

Ahmed's eyes seemed enormous to Reut, much larger than she'd remembered, full of innocence and purity. This observation cost her yet another delay in her great race: she felt she couldn't leave without apologizing to him and offering a proper goodbye.

"*Merci,*" Reut said, shaking his hand. "Very nice to meet you."

"You too, mademoiselle!"

"And, um . . . sorry about before. Maybe I—" Reut fell silent. She wanted to explain herself. Finally, she just said, "*Merci*! And good luck with everything! *Au revoir*!"

"*Au revoir*, Re-ut," Ahmed said, watching her as she disappeared into the distance.

CHARLES DE GAULLE AIRPORT

FLUSHED and panting, Reut finally found the correct counter and a young man greeted her. He seemed like a child to Reut, twenty years old at most. "Madame, *bonjour!*"

"*Voilà!*" She offered her documents in lieu of a greeting. "And, if you don't mind, please hurry, although it's probably already too—"

"Hmmm . . ." said the boy, "Would madame prefer a middle seat or an aisle seat? Unfortunately no window seats are left."

"What does that matter right now?!" she barked. Then, "Aisle. Aisle seat would be fine."

"An aisle seat . . . *d'accord!*" The boy spent a few seconds contemplating the screen, clicking his tongue like a horse trainer. "All right." As he handed her the documents, he added, "Madame, next trip I recommend not showing up at the last moment. You were lucky this time. Your flight is delayed by an hour and a half. But surely you'll agree it is unwise to rely on flights being delayed?"

Feeling lighter without her large suitcase, Reut moved briskly to her next destination. Now that she'd learned about the delay, her adrenaline vanished. Her irritation, on the other hand, was intact—for her needless rushing, and for the young horse trainer. She must look terrible now! She worried that her aggravation was clearly visible through her makeup, giving her an aged, haggard look. She had to get to a bathroom mirror and freshen up.

Reut spotted the bathroom sign and headed over. Fortunately, it was very close. Unfortunately, many other women needed it just as badly as she did. Before she could even decide if she had the patience to wait, Reut joined the line.

Since childhood, Reut enjoyed watching people as they waited in line. She did this artfully, aware that staring had its perils. It wasn't hard to pick up clues about the woman in front of her. She appeared more or less the same age as Reut, equipped with money and free time, which she liked to devote to herself. And she cared about herself deeply, a fact evident in her tasteful clothes, skillfully applied nail polish, and carefully coiffed hair (freshly dyed auburn, straightened with a hot iron, little curls at the end). Though Reut was generally satisfied with her own appearance, she couldn't help but feel curiosity mixed with envy as she observed perfect (too perfect?) women at airports. Who were they? What was going through their minds?

Three steps forward in the shadow of the perfect woman, a dose of tentative optimism . . . but no! They stopped again. The line didn't budge. That was it. Reut abandoned the line for the toilets and waited for a sink to free up. In any case, the real reason she'd come to the bathroom in the first place was to touch up her appearance. As she waited, her eyes fixed on a girl, seventeen years old at most, who'd taken over the second sink to the right. Watching, first with impatience, then with sorrow, Reut followed the girl's meticulous scrubbing of her hands, with no awareness of the passage of time.

Four or five times—Reut wasn't sure—the girl added more soap, then scrubbed carefully once again. Even from a distance, her hands seemed to be bright red from the boiling water. They were the hands of an elderly woman, attached to a young body. Wrinkled hands, worn raw from incessant washing. When she finally turned off the faucet, the girl quickly dried her fingers and left, eyes glued to the floor. Reut looked away and hurried over to grab the free sink. At least she could see that for herself things weren't as bad as she'd imagined.

After a brisk walk that bordered on a run, Reut tracked down gate F2. She paused to look over the seats and her flight mates. An odd sensation took hold of her: the departure gate wasn't as crowded as she'd expected. Retracing her steps, she searched for the departure screen. The calm atmosphere of F2 appeared suspicious to her. Indeed, the screen showed that her flight was delayed by another twenty minutes.

"What's going on here today?" she asked herself.

Flopping down, defeated, she pulled a bottle of water from her bag to alleviate her terrible thirst. Then she let her eyes close. The tension at the airport, the shouting, the running, the translation work at the brasserie beforehand—they all piled up. She closed her eyes for about ten minutes, giving into darkness, slowly sinking deeper. Then her eyes opened, and the outside world rushed inward. Beside the airline counter, she noticed an incipient boarding line. She knew well what this meant. Soon a swell of people rose hotly from their seats, swooping in to find their places in the most important line of all. Following suit, Reut managed to snag a reasonable spot: only about twenty people separated her from the counter. For the first time since this morning, she felt a welcome excitement in anticipating her arrival in Puglia.

AIRPLANE

REUT smiled mechanically at the pair of flight attendants standing at the front of the plane. Then she advanced down the aisle, evading the curious faces of people who had already taken their seats. She was the first to arrive at her row, and she wondered about the identity of her seatmates. Ideally: a couple who wanted to watch a movie together or sleep through the entire flight. More likely: a pair of lovers or best friends with a rich pool of conversation topics.

Both possibilities evaporated less than a minute after she buckled her seatbelt. Seatmate Number 1 was a young woman of small stature, pale and screechy voiced. She addressed Reut with wary politeness, asking her to stand up so that she could get to her seat. Reut hurried to oblige, feeling the woman's mousy eyes on her—they seemed to be asking, *What in the world made you think it was a good idea to buckle up before your fellow passengers arrived?* At the same time, the eyes confided, *I'm having a terrible day.*

By the time Reut sat back down, her neighbor had already adopted the standard airplane napping position: arms crossed, knees bent against the seat ahead of hers, head leaned clumsily against the window. Reut watched her for a few moments, following the way her mouth went limp and defenseless, as if summoning dreams. There was something about people sleeping in public places that had always charmed Reut, awakening her anthropological curiosity: Where did they get the audacity not only to present their truest selves to a clump of strangers, but to relinquish all control by surrendering to unconsciousness?

In an instant, the frantic movements in the airplane aisle surged into the corner of her eye and the rustling of passengers invaded her ears. Quickly, she pulled out her research book and opened it to a random page. She knew she wouldn't be able to read a single word: the book's sole purpose at that moment was as an object she could focus upon, a talisman to protect her vision from the scene of people boarding the plane.

Reut looked around, trying to understand what was going on. The plane seemed ready to take off, but for some reason they were lingering on the ground. She returned her book to her bag. She felt bored, exposed. She pulled out her cellphone and checked for anything new in social media and her inbox. Then she clicked on the browser app and looked blankly at the search window. She was out of ideas, but she was reluctant to put away the phone and surrender to doing nothing. She typed in: "Polignano a Mare what to see." Various hits emerged. She clicked on one of them, scanned the contents, and then left the app.

She placed the phone on her right thigh, leaned her head back, and rested for a moment. Then: inspiration! She typed: "Aliza Shor."

In a flash, countless results appeared on the screen. Reut clicked on the first one, the *New York Times Book Review*, no less.

"The Female Reincarnation of Kafka," the headline pronounced.

"Aliza Shor, a long-awaited new voice in literature," the subtitle determined.

Scrunching her eyebrows together, Reut took in these overblown assessments. Then, her heart rate intensifying, she scrolled down to the piece itself: a moving, sophisticated, occasionally brilliant book—Reut soon learned from critic Malcolm O'Brien—a quintessential feminist text, a personal and painful autobiography that hinted toward transcendence. Scrolling to the reviewer's analysis, Reut struggled to follow O'Brien's logic and found herself within a suffocating tangle of praise. Her mind wandered from the article to her own lips, which bothered her just as much.

On her bottom lip—there, on the right—an irritating swelling. A gentle peeling, an attempt to smooth it out. A sharp turn inward, to the inside of her lip—another dry lump, another peeling, deeper this time. Her lips were like an unkempt lawn: they needed to be trimmed, manicured, policed. But the work never ended. Another bit of skin pulled off, but no amount of peeling satisfied her. Mindlessly staring at her phone. Then she jerked her hand away, startled by the male voice that emerged from the airplane's sound system. Ugh! She couldn't be bothered to watch the safety video now. Her eyes returned to the article, and she continued to pull at her lips. In a few sweet moments, her lips were smoothed, with no bits of dry skin peeking out. And yet, Reut aspired to perfection: she thought there was still a little broken skin in an inner, hidden corner of her upper lip. She tried to push the urge away, fighting as hard as she could to return her attention to O'Brien, but all of a sudden that small, evasive split of skin became the only thing in the world that mattered to her.

Blood. A burning sensation. Reut quickly covered the broken spot with her finger, which only exacerbated the sting. Removing the finger, she looked with indifference at the small spot of blood that had stained it, then returned the finger to the exposed area, then looked at it again. Glistening blood. Her indifference evaporated, and disgust and fury at herself took its place. Shoving her hand between her crossed legs, she returned to the phone's browser. She didn't know how to stop. Another article about Aliza, more praise, the *Washington Post* this time! She needed to go to the bathroom but was unable to detach herself from the screen.

Then, blessedly, the flight attendant spoke to her: "Madame, please straighten your seatback and switch your phone to airplane mode. We're about to take off."

Reut chewed vigorously on a piece of gum as the airplane took to the sky. She was extremely sensitive to inner-ear pressure during takeoff. As the plane leveled out, she began her usual routine: going to the bathroom, reading a bit, resting. Then: unlocking her tray table, picking at the food, letting her tray be cleared and accepting a hot beverage. Reut opted for murky coffee, which she also barely touched. As she waited for the attendant to clear away her cup, she watched as a frequent economy-class occurrence played itself out. She followed the course of the argument, knowing well how loud it would get.

The hostile exchange of words took place between two nearby passengers, Woman A and Woman B. The similarity between them: both were born and raised in Paris. The difference between them: one wore a fashionable haircut from a Le Marais stylist, the other a hijab.

After debating for a while whether or not to confront Woman B, Woman A turned around to speak her truth: "Excuse me, madame, sorry to interrupt, but my husband isn't feeling well. If you could please ask your children to lower their voices that would be a great help."

Woman B, putting on a hurt expression: "My children are fine. They're playing."

Woman A, enunciating her words: "I see. Perhaps they could play a little more quietly in a public place. This airplane is crowded and you see my husband is trying to get some sleep. I'm sure you understand."

Woman B, addressing Woman A as *tu* rather than the more respectful *vous*: "You want me to shut them up, madame?" In the absence of an immediate response, Woman B turned to face her two children, urging them cheerfully, "*Kamlu, ya hilwin. Ilabu, ilabu.* Go on, sweethearts, play, play."

Woman A, flabbergasted, never expected Woman B to be so disrespectful. She turned to her husband, who gave her nothing more than a feeble caress on the thigh and a request that she calm down.

But how could she be treated this way? She would not let Woman B and her savage children get away with this! Turning around sharply, she spoke to Woman B again, emphasizing her *vous*, eyes glimmering with fury: "Yes, I want you to tell them to shut up. And, tell him—yes, him—to stop kicking my seat, and—"

"Shut your mouth, madame, you should be ashamed of yourself!" Woman B shouted. "Leave my children alone, you—"

As the two carried on, Reut thought she heard someone addressing her in Hebrew. She turned her head quickly, assuming she'd only imagined it. But then, from the seat across the aisle, she heard more words in Hebrew, spoken with a heavy French accent: "Awful, isn't it?"

"What? Ummm . . ." Reut mumbled, confused by the Hebrew. "Excuse me? I didn't hear you."

"That . . ." the woman said, peppering every vowel with a nasal French twang, "what's going on there, all the—the way people behave, *impossible*!"

"Oh, yes," Reut murmured. "Definitely."

While Reut considered what to say next, the woman turned away. When she turned back to face Reut she informed her: "*Wai, wai*, look at them—ah! *C'est terrible*! I don't understand what's going on there."

"The noise is bothering her," Reut said dully and fell silent. She could have added more, but she hesitated; the

woman seemed too bouncy, too cheerful, leaving Reut unde-
cided if she wanted to engage with her. What would she even
say? What would this woman make of Reut's mixed emotions? Of her agreement, in principle, with Woman A while
also feeling disgusted by her? Of the uncomfortable pity she
felt toward Woman B for experiencing Woman A's attack,
which she must have been familiar with from other situations
in her life. A shared language alongside an unbridgeable foreignness: cultural condescension needed no words.

With the woman's eyes still transfixed on her, aching for
conversation, Reut finally said, "Your Hebrew is very good."

"Oh, *merciii*! No, no, but—not at all. *C'est terrible*. Still
so many mistakes!"

"Not at all," Reut assured her, offering the woman a generous smile. "By the way, how could you tell I speak Hebrew?"

"I don't know. It was just obvious! With the flight attendant, when you asked about the meal. Sure, it was clear."

"So you're saying my accent is strong?" Reut asked slowly,
so that the woman could understand.

"Super strong."

Reut leaned down to search for some candy in her bag,
hoping that by turning away she would put an end to the
casual conversation. Though she found the woman pleasant
enough, the idea of resting for the remainder of the flight
appealed to her more. But, switching between French and
Hebrew, the young woman showed insatiable interest in
Reut: Who was she? What was she doing in France? How
long has she been there? At first, the barrage of questions

disarmed Reut. Each answer she provided only led to more follow-up questions. She wasn't used to talking so much so fast, and about herself, no less. And yet, after six minutes of interrogation, the woman's relentless curiosity began to charm her. It was familiar, homey. That Israeli spontaneity, that tendency to force strangers into becoming friends, the kind of things Reut tended to turn up her nose at, though sometimes, when she was far away from Israel, they warmed her soul.

Without noticing, Reut lost herself completely in the conversation. But, now and then, she also pulled away, evicting herself from her own body and transmuting into an exterior Reut, curiously watching the talkative, liberated Reut who let out the occasional exuberant laugh that faded tenderly. She was completely herself, relaxed and nonjudgmental. No words were inappropriate. In these kinds of moments, Reut couldn't help but be impressed by the way such a cliché proved true before her eyes: the power of language to influence a person's demeanor, their sense of decorum. Reut had not a shadow of a doubt that the conversation would have been entirely different if it had taken place solely in French. The cultural norms rooted in the language along with the barricade between *vous* and *tu* would have thwarted spontaneity, censoring any potential for instant intimacy.

From the handful of questions Reut had managed to get in, she'd gathered a few important details about her fellow traveler: her name was Julie Amzaleg, twenty-nine years old, originally from Nice, newly immigrated from France to

Israel, recently engaged to a man from Jerusalem. Despite the challenges of adapting to the mentality, the language, and her new life, Julie pointed out how happy she was with her choice, and how much more at ease she felt in Tel Aviv than she had in France. "My philosophy," she said, "is that life is tough everywhere. You only need to choose where you want to be and who you want to be with when it gets tough."

Julie returned to her line of questioning. It took over two minutes before Reut had a chance to ask her to explain exactly what she'd meant by that cryptic statement. Julie was glad to do so, switching to French for the purpose. The central imperative of her life philosophy, she explained, was to be bold, to look beyond the familiar to be able to choose for oneself one's own challenging life. According to her, most people were too enslaved by their own fears to dare to do this. And this was very sad indeed, since only by choosing their own difficult life could they make peace with it. Her conclusion: people constantly seek to adapt to reality instead of creating a new reality for themselves.

Reut couldn't help but challenge Julie on her creed. She protested that she had chosen to live in Paris rather than in Israel or New York; that she was the one who'd chosen to uproot her life, say goodbye to her friends and her research, become a full-time translator, and settle in Paris with Jean-Claude. It was all her choice. She was completely free to choose differently. Jean-Claude even made a point of telling her that before she'd decided. So why was she occasionally disturbed by restlessness or some other elusive emotion? She'd chosen her own challenge—where was her great happiness?

When Julie asked for more details about the nature of her challenges, Reut was unable to give any. Everything was fine, more or less. At least there was no specific problem she considered unique or insurmountable. Ultimately, the only answer Reut could give Julie was, "Nothing exactly, just life . . . is complicated."

When the airplane touched down in Italy, Reut felt a pleasant fatigue. It was the sensation she experienced whenever she'd had an extended conversation with a new acquaintance. That obligation to be more attentive than usual, to engage fully, to maintain eye contact—it required an unaccustomed degree of concentration.

Reut loved feeling this specific fatigue, that post-conversation moment, in which both parties felt satisfied about their own self-exposure, a temporary closeness between strangers. Both would mull over insights gained, savoring a fleeting overlap of lives that soon enough diverged as before, each to its familiar path. How odd was the power of a single conversation—so brief when compared to life's expanse—to carve into her soul another flash of memory that would surface inexplicably from time to time, carrying her forward.

PART III

PUGLIA

TRATTORIA

Reut searched the train platform for Jean-Claude. He was nowhere to be found, but her eyes continued to scan arduously, like the floodlights of a tired lighthouse.

The length of the journey from Bari Airport to Polignano a Mare had surpassed Reut's expectations: the train was late to arrive, then inexplicably broke down. On top of this, Reut's body refused to let her fall asleep. How she begged it to comply, to let her head rest for just a few minutes. Soon she'd have to be nice to everyone—say hello to Jean-Claude, hello to Grigoryev, hello to some strangers she'd be sharing the summer home with. But her day was over. She felt like a mop wrung of every last drop of small talk. She'd spent all her smiles on Julie.

Tired and irritated, Reut dialed her husband's number.

"Where *are* you?! I don't see you anywhere."

"Oh, *chérie*! Did you arrive already?"

"Yes, I—" She fell silent, bit her lips. "Where are you?"

"I'll be right there. I saw the train was delayed, so I was waiting here, at the bar next door. I'll just pay and—"

Jean-Claude hung up abruptly, and Reut walked to an empty bench nearby, dragging her suitcase slowly behind her.

She sat down and let her eyes glaze over the train tracks before her. She was beyond anger or disappointment, resigned to waiting for him to show up. But gradually, unknowingly, she ceased even to wait, ceased all consideration of what she was doing there: she was Reut, simply Reut, sitting on a bench in an unfamiliar station, opening her body to the welcoming breeze of the Adriatic Sea.

When Jean-Claude finally appeared, it took her a few moments to react appropriately. She greeted him right away, of course, but it was some other, exterior Reut who did the greeting. The real Reut was still imbibing the Pugliese air and the stillness.

"You're so tan," she pointed out mechanically, handing him her suitcase.

Jean-Claude grabbed it and moved toward the gate with that speedy seal walk of his. How she used to hate his asymmetrical feet, each pointing in a different direction. It took her so many years to stop despising them and even, occasionally, to not notice them at all.

Tethered to his shadow, she followed him out of the station in near silence. She came to a halt in an alleyway, fixing Jean-Claude with a look of astonishment that was not yet anger. For the first time since he'd started dictating their pace, Reut noticed her heavy breathing; she was nearly running. Panting, she asked him why they were in such a hurry. Where was he taking her? She'd told him she was exhausted, she wanted to stay in that night at Grigoryev's place and rest.

"You can rest later," Jean-Claude declared. "We've got an entire week to rest. But now, come on, they're waiting for us."

"*Waiting*? Where?! No, no! Absolutely not, look at me. I can't possibly go out looking like this."

"You look lovely," Jean-Claude mumbled, glancing at his watch. "We really don't have time for this right now."

Reut rolled her eyes in frustration. She let Jean-Claude rest his hand against her lower back, and pushing slightly, he sped her up again.

After many more steps, Jean-Claude announced, all atwitter, "*Chérie*! Look where we are! Look—look at that!"

A few short seconds of astonishment, absorbing the beauty of the darkening houses, and then he slowed down a bit, wrapping his arm around her body. "You'll see where I'm taking you soon, Tutu. Mikhail says it's one of his favorite spots. Any minute and we'll be there—it, it should be right here . . ."

"*Bien*," Reut grumbled, too tired to argue.

But then she saw, and her taut nerves unraveled.

For the first time since leaving the train station, Reut looked around her, truly *looked*, taking in the spectacle before her: a perfect night, fit for a painting, one that shed any kitschiness as soon as she experienced it, became part of it. Through charmed eyes, she observed the beauty of the Italian alleyways, all those stone houses she'd expected to see—in fact, *had* seen in pictures—but not like this: not built into each other in this inimitable way, not lit by this white and gold arc that the sheen of street lights struck *just so*. Those green shutters! The cracks! And the narrow stairs, and the wandering vines! Marvelous sounds penetrated her ears, the sounds of a resort town, not those of a city. Cascading conversations, an assortment of voices of different volumes coming together to form a pleasant rustle. The smells! Aromas of the sea and seared fish scented the air, battling for precedence.

"What a wonderful place . . ." Reut mumbled, partly to Jean-Claude and partly to herself. A wave of joy came over her.

"Yes," he agreed a few moments later, his expression tense. After a beat, he added, "But it's supposed to be here, the . . . wait, it's—No. This doesn't make sense."

"Should we ask someone?" Reut asked without really asking. She already knew his answer.

"*Putain*, it's supposed to be right here! One second, let me check. It's . . . Come on, where's that sign?!"

Another five minutes of searching without accepting help go by, and then success! Grigoryev's favorite trattoria: La Casa Di Giuseppe. The trattoria's sign was well hidden. Jean-Claude concluded that it was no wonder he'd passed it by without noticing, and also, that this must be a restaurant frequented only by those *in the know.*

The owner, Giuseppe, greeted them at the door. He was just about to step outside for a smoke with a customer Reut thought looked a bit shady.

"Where's that suitcase?" Giuseppe roared in the local Bari dialect. A grin lighting up his face, he tossed his cigarette, took hold of her luggage, and hoisted it onto the corner of the bar.

Reut was riveted by Giuseppe's movements. Much like her experience with the picturesque alleyways, Reut found that Giuseppe perfectly embodied her ideal of "authentic trattoria owner." While still surprising her with his specificity, he enriched her imaginary blueprint of Italy.

Reut needed only a few seconds to compose a rich profile of Giuseppe that went much deeper than his gut, tan, and thick hair: her eyes saw a man of strong, multitudinous character. A hard worker equally proficient at enjoying life. A man who had encountered many struggles but had always made light of his burdens, infecting even the bitterest of people with his joy. Reut rarely met the type of person she made Giuseppe out to be, but she had a natural affection for such figures, yearning to immerse herself in their laughter.

On his way back from the bar, Giuseppe joked around with one of the servers, slapping his back. As he approached Jean-Claude and Reut he cried, "*C'est bon*!" Then, in English, with a palpable local accent, "Massimo will take care of you."

Reut was puzzled. How did he know to address them in French?

Anyway, when Jean-Claude addressed Massimo in English, his accent left no room for doubt. "We are joining friends," he said with authority. "Reservation under the name Grigoryev. Mikhail Grigoryev."

"*Un minuto*, let me check." Massimo opened his reservation book, wheezing as he scanned it. "*Eccoci qua*!" he finally declared. "Please come."

Massimo led them into a charming courtyard overlooking the rocky bay of Polignano a Mare. As soon as she walked in, Reut recognized the celebrated author and Katya's slender back across from him. She did not, however, recognize the man beside Katya.

That back belonged to Pavel Grigoryev, Mikhail's older brother by two years. Though Reut knew he would be there, her first sight of him bewildered her. Smiling at Pavel before the double-kiss ritual, Reut could not ignore how terribly close to Katya he sat or the way his arm coiled around her waist. More striking even was Mikhail, whose cheerful expression showed no concern for the obvious intimacy between his wife and his brother.

"Pavel," Mikhail hummed as Jean-Claude and Reut took their seats, "I'd like to introduce you to this beautiful woman. Reut . . . Reut is a translator. A historian. She's currently studying the significance of myths in, umm—in the time of the American Civil War—am I explaining this right, Reut? Please correct me if—"

"Yes," she assented, "that's exactly right."

"*Alors*, Reut," Mikhail continued, raising his wineglass, "first of all, I'd like to say how delighted I am that you could finally join us. *Vot*. Unfortunately, we have reduced numbers here tonight. Bernard and Marion are at their own private celebration—a first wedding anniversary. Ha! The woman who got Bernard to settle down . . . A miracle worker!" After another hearty sip of wine, Mikhail raised his glass yet again. "At any rate, I'm glad to introduce you to my brother. My dear brother, Pavel. We never see each other unless I come to Italy. Paris isn't beautiful enough for him to visit." He sipped again, cleared his throat. "So Pavel is—well, you'll see for yourself soon enough, when we get home—Pavel is a gifted painter. *Vot* . . . he also specializes in antique furniture restoration."

"*Enchanté*," said Reut, trying to assume a casual expression. And yet she felt restrained. This playful formality only exacerbated her self-awareness. Every gesture and word were carefully chosen. When Pavel said nothing, she asked hesitantly, piercing his silence, "Do you . . . speak French?"

"I do," he replied, smiling mysteriously. His smile was clearly intended for Mikhail and Katya, Reut noticed. Frazzled, Reut rose from her seat, asking Mikhail if he could point her to the bathroom.

"Yes, it's—" he began, then, "One moment, Reut, before Massimo comes back, please tell me, is there anything you don't eat? I can't remember at our last meal together if—"

"She eats everything," Jean-Claude quickly assured him. "No issue with keeping kosher."

"Mmm," the author replied. "Because, you see, Giuseppe and I have a little ritual: I show up and he takes charge. He brings anything that's fresh and we share it all. How does that sound?"

"Sounds great."

On her way to the bathroom, Reut had a chance to take a closer look at the trattoria—the mismatched decor, the colors, one wall covered with photographs of previous diners and the other crowded with wine bottles—it stole Reut's heart in an instant. Near the entrance to the courtyard, she noticed a small station where one of the chefs was preparing *orecchiette*, a Pugliese pasta named for its resemblance to small ears. Reut watched the chef for a few moments as if he were a street performer, then walked on, smiling.

All the tables inside were full. A mélange of languages blended together, spoken by people sharing nothing but a decision to celebrate the evening in the same place. It was a matter of principle, Reut believed: anyone less than happy in such a picturesque locale was failing at something. Indeed, most of the diners were joyfully laughing and raising their voices, immersed in the same enthusiastic search for connection, with smatterings of small talk to enrich the memory of their vacations.

Reut couldn't help but be infected by the good cheer of the place, her mood completely transformed in the brief time away from the table. Now she no longer cared whether or not she looked good, whether or not she sounded proper, whether or not they'd have something to talk about, whether or not they'd have fun, because she decided that she would have fun, that she would not feel tired, that her stomach would not hurt—and that was that!

And, in fact, during the nearly three hours their quintet spent at the trattoria, Reut was in top form, flirting indiscriminately, questioning people with ease, opining elegantly. She stopped prattling only to listen, eat, or sip her wine. She drank a lot, to Jean-Claude's dismay. He signaled her to slow down three times during the meal, and three times she waved him off with a laugh. Jean-Claude himself drank plenty, like the rest of their party: they polished off four carafes of the house wine and two more rounds of Amaro for digestion's sake. The liqueur was refreshing and fennel based, a typical Pugliese flavor.

The conversations whirling around Reut soon turned to a slew of fascinating anecdotes about the Grigoryev family. The stories seemed completely fantastical, astoundingly far from her own range of experience: from Saint Petersburg to Moscow to Paris, the Grigoryev family lore arose from the snow-blown revolutionary world of the Russian intelligentsia and the Bolshevik party. Reut had trouble believing that these stories were truly part of the tapestry of memory of the people sitting around her. They sounded so foreign, so romantic, so removed from her childhood memories from Israel. This cultural abyss, served with a side of light conversation, couldn't help but amaze and charm Reut over the course of the dinner: a degree of difference that changed everything and nothing at all.

During their after-dinner stroll to the writer's house, Reut mentally reviewed his familial anecdotes. She drew up the outlines of the stories, filling in the colors in her mind, yearning to learn more about the dramatic cast: the mother—French, a devout Catholic who died suddenly of pneumonia when Mikhail was four; the father—a prominent figure in the Bolshevik party, a true painter until he became swept up by Stalin's ideological constraints; the paternal grandmother—a strong woman and masterful storyteller who raised the two brothers and their half-sister from their father's first marriage; the maternal great-grandfather—a renowned linguist and a staunch opponent of Lenin who was banished from the Soviet Union in 1922 with other intellectuals on one of the legendary "philosophers' ships." As a side note, Pavel mentioned that the family was strictly forbidden from bringing up the ship or the great-grandfather's name. If anyone ever did, Pavel informed them, his father would go wild.

The tales of the Grigoryev family inflamed Reut's curiosity about Pavel. Though he spoke readily throughout the meal, his identity remained mysteriously obscure. Something in his expression deterred Reut. When he spoke, his eyes almost never met hers. They darted around heatedly, then suddenly fixed on a random point in space. Occasionally he smiled, but only when least expected. When he did, she offered her own smile in return, diluted with fear and curiosity. What was he thinking? Reut didn't dare voice this question, or the others that came to mind, fearing they would be perceived as overly invasive. Was he married? Did he have a family? Why didn't he live in Paris like Mikhail, and what stopped him from visiting?

But perhaps, more than anything else, Reut wanted to know the exact nature of his relationship with Katya, his brother's wife. Dinner was dominated by the perplexing scene of Katya leaning her head against Pavel's shoulder, the two of them caressing furtively and exchanging giddy intimate glances. Katya and Mikhail also exchanged grins and brief kisses after the writer joined his wife's side of the table, wrapping an arm around her as if to say "You're mine"— though very much letting her belong publicly to another, his brother, and seeming to enjoy it.

Everything seemed permissible within this threesome; gestures of affection limitless. There had to be something between Katya and Pavel beyond "a friendship that goes back to preschool days," Reut was sure of it. Yet she doubted— or had trouble believing—that Katya and Pavel had even, in fact, known each other since preschool. If the two of them were the same age, that meant that the glamorous, flawless Ekaterina was two years older than her husband.

Long live makeup! All hail plastic surgery!

THE FIRST NIGHT

THE group's stroll delivered them to Mikhail's place. Reut hadn't paid any attention to the route. She was utterly immersed in her thoughts and happy to know she would soon have some time to herself. The desire to be alone sharpened to an acute need when the group paused to chat in the foyer. Everyone looked so pleased with themselves and the small talk they were spinning. Their night, it seemed, had just begun.

Reut bent to remove her shoes, and Jean-Claude's cheerful voice boomed through the foyer. When Reut stood up, she saw him standing with his arms crossed in front of the brothers and Katya, his face lit up. Her stomach cramped. He's happy. How wonderful! So where was this happiness hiding earlier? Why the infuriating eclipse that had overcome him? Reut had noticed Jean-Claude's sour expression back at the trattoria, of course. She also knew that he knew she'd noticed it, and that he was irritated even more by her indifference.

But Jean-Claude didn't realize that his sullenness did agitate Reut, if belatedly. It had been incubating in her mind since dinner, waiting for his glowing smile to bring the memory to the surface. As Reut recalled the look on his face, it seemed to her a personal attack. It was as if it had been saying: *You're too happy, you're too carefree, it's like I don't even know you.*

And now that she felt she had been squelched, becoming quiet and genial, order was restored. Jean-Claude had arisen, reclaiming his crown, ready to delight his friends once more. Reut hated these thoughts and her own bitter self for entertaining them. But Jean-Claude's glumness at the trattoria had to be a result of her overt happiness. No other explanation was possible.

Hesitantly advancing toward the group, Reut wondered how long they'd keep yammering on. Pausing behind Katya, she decided to wait another minute before announcing that she was off to bed.

Twenty seconds later—the rattle of a key being slipped into the door.

"Ah!" Reut jumped, startled out of her exhaustion. "Who's that?!"

And then Bernard and Marion came over the threshold, embracing and giggling, elegantly attired. Bernard sported a tailored summer suit over a blinding white shirt unbuttoned to reveal his chest. Marion was dashing in a tight gold dress and shockingly high stilettos. Neither of them was especially attractive, but to Reut they still looked like a pair of movie stars.

"*Buona sera!*" Jean-Claude greeted them first.

"So, did you get bored?" Mikhail asked as he walked over to Bernard and slapped his back. "How was it?"

"*Écoute*—" Bernard murmured.

"How was it—" Marion cut him off. "It was . . . incredible! Just—*mon chouchou*, give me your phone—you've got to see this amazing place he took me to, it's just—well, *chéri*, are you giving it to me?—Ha! Everything just looks better through his camera. One moment . . ."

As Bernard extracted the phone from his pocket, Marion spotted Reut behind Katya's back. "*Bonjour*! I didn't see you there—Reut, no?"

"Yes," Reut confirmed, automatically adding, "I've heard a lot about you." She kissed Marion twice, the height difference caused by the stilettos making her feel fantastically clumsy; another two kisses with Bernard, who, to her surprise, held her arm intimately. Several pairs of eyes carefully followed these greetings. Everyone in the hallway was in high spirits.

"What do you say, shall we go to the living room? A little whiskey before bed? Oh, well, there's also fabulous vodka for anyone who prefers that . . ." Without waiting for a response, Mikhail bounded off to the living room, convinced that the others would follow (they did). He called Reut's name as she kept pace. When she was near, he asked more tenderly, "Reut, *chérie*, do you like vodka? Come, have a taste of what Pavel got for us. It's exquisite."

Reut didn't want to stay. She was too tired to drink, but etiquette obligated her to join the writer at the liquor cabinet. Graciously accepting the glass he poured for her, she thanked him and took a small sip. Indeed, the vodka was very good, she told him immediately. And surprisingly, she meant it. Though Reut didn't typically like hard liquor, the taste of that vodka was different than what she was used to. It was spiced with subtle sweetness and slid easily down her throat—or had Reut just sipped too little? She quickly gulped down some more to be sure.

To Reut's dismay, Jean-Claude and Bernard joined them at the liquor cabinet just as she took her big second sip. Bernard rushed to make a comment that Reut found all too predictable among men: "Ha-ha, your wife sure can drink!"

"Yes, she . . ." Jean-Claude mumbled. Resting a hand firmly on her shoulder, he added, "Tutu, you're letting loose tonight, aren't you?"

Reut said she would be right back. It was close to midnight and no one seemed keen on ending the party and the living room was bustling. Mikhail put on some music and told his friends that the voice they were hearing belonged to Roberto Murolo, one of the "most gifted interpreters" of Neapolitan poetry.

Reut enjoyed Murolo's enchanting serenade but was aware of its dangerous effect on her: her body slowly sank into the couch and her eyelids grew heavy. She sat up quickly, cleared her throat, and said to no one in particular, "I'll be right back."

Reut had no idea where she was meant to sleep. The house, she soon discovered, was a sort of sophisticated maze sprawling over three stories. Where to go? She sighed with impatience. She had to be alone. The last thing she intended to do was return to the living room for help. She couldn't be seen this way. Vodka, wine, digestifs, and pasta made for an unwise combination in hindsight.

Gripped by nausea and exhaustion, Reut searched desperately. But when she saw it, she recognized it almost instantly; she felt relief at the familiar sight of Jean-Claude's button-down spread over a chair, his leather briefcase placed neatly on a dresser and his books on a desk.

The bedroom wasn't enormous, but it wasn't small, either. Even in the grip of her stomachache, she took in its magic: high ceiling, large windows, drawn burgundy drapes. The furniture was minimalist but elegant: an armoire, a desk, a bed, and two dressers, all fashioned of wood and a few pieces intricately ornamented. A worn lampshade dangling from the ceiling appeared, like the furniture, handmade.

Reut was drawn to two large and impressive oil paintings on the walls. Were they Pavel's? Quite possibly. She examined the one over the bed, then plopped down. Sitting up with her eyes shut, Reut tried to allow her body a quick rest. Her palms were open wide; taut, alert fingers still grasping consciousness. She knew if she leaned back she'd be down until morning. Her entire bedtime routine lay ahead of her, and she wasn't about to abandon it.

That's it, she would get up. She would open her eyes and stand, now. They remained closed. Her fingers slowly curled as she let down her defenses and colors flickered past her eyes as her vision dimmed. A strange, nebulous thought flickered too, the seed of a dream slowing her breathing, softening it, deepening it. Her neck was suddenly heavy and falling behind her.

Her eyes snapped open as if from a nightmare—she stood up.

Reut left the bedroom with a nightgown, clean underwear, and two pouches of toiletries. Thanks to her wanderings, she already knew where the nearest bathroom was. On her way there, she heard howling from the living room. *What's wrong with them? Are they children?* Reut didn't want to think about it. She wanted to wash up, in silence. A few steps later and she was there. The door closing behind her, the lock turning, her eyes meeting the mirror.

She removed her blouse, then her floral sweatpants. It hurt to bend over. She tossed the clothes onto the counter and was about to get in the shower, but then quickly went back, gripped by an odd sensation that if she left her clothes lying around something bad might happen. She knew she was being paranoid, but when she got urges like these she typically indulged them to quiet her panic.

After folding her clothes and placing them back on the counter—neatly this time—the mirror met Reut's eyes again. Reut looked at herself—first her neck, which she hadn't been pleased with lately, then her breasts—with the cold gaze of a physician no longer surprised by anything she saw. She stepped into the shower. She slid the glass door shut and turned to face the faucets.

The shock of the hot water hit her body. She turned the faucet. Now the water was boiling. She held the showerhead against her chest for a while, then sprayed it on her face like a sprinkler. What a marvelous sensation! She felt as if she'd just returned from a long hike, her body smelly and sticky, her hair tangled and mussed, and now she had finally found water. It expunged the grime at once, remolding her old self into perfection that would last until her hair dried.

Reut stepped out of the shower and wrapped a towel around herself. She wiped the steam from the mirror, glancing at patches of her reflection in the blurred glass. Her mascara was smeared, but she didn't care. She felt happy, awake. The most important nightly ritual was about to begin.

Humming a made-up tune, Reut pulled out soap and makeup remover from her pouch and began to thoroughly clean her face. Then, eyes half-closed, she groped around for a face towel. She held it to her face for a moment, then dabbed it in order—first her cheeks, then her forehead—relishing the routine. A night serum (an essential foundation), moisturizer (applied in round, repetitive motions), eye cream (just a touch, patted in gently). Throughout the ritual, her focus never wavered. She enjoyed touching herself and having time alone with her body in an unfamiliar, well-lit bathroom. Time was entirely different here than in Paris: no rush, no guilt, nothing more urgent than the present moment and her self-care.

Reut closed the bathroom door carefully behind her. Her hair was still damp, her body clad in satin. Sauntering back to the bedroom, she thought of whether the group downstairs might still be partying in the living room. The answer soon arrived.

"*Salut!*" Jean-Claude greeted her bitterly as soon as she opened the door.

"Hi?" she mumbled guardedly.

"Where were you?"

Reut looked confused. "I was taking a shower."

"*D'accord.*"

And with that, the conversation ended. Sitting on the edge of the bed, his back slightly hunched, Jean-Claude returned his eyes to his cellphone. Whom could he be texting at this hour? A mystery. Reut remained in the doorway, watching him uncomfortably. She hoped he'd cut it out and talk to her. He was already in his pajamas: a white T-shirt for his wine gut, and a pair of Calvin Kleins.

Jean-Claude's indifference snuffed Reut's spirits. Suddenly, she craved a small gesture of affection, to rest her head on his lap and let him run his hands through her hair. She walked slowly to the bed and sat close to him, nonchalantly. Jean-Claude noted her presence but did not shift. His eyes remained fixed on the screen. Bored, Reut tilted her head to see what he was writing. Emailing a colleague—just as she had assumed. Reut never doubted Jean-Claude's skill in hiding from her any romantic escapade he might have at the university.

But still, if this was just a colleague, why now, so late, in the middle of their important vacation? Jean-Claude occasionally worked in the evenings, but now it was infuriating!

"Is something wrong?" she asked, placing a hand on his thigh.

Six seconds without a response. Reut pulled her hand away.

A few seconds later, Jean-Claude mumbled, "It's, um . . . one second."

In a few more seconds, he quickly patted Reut's thigh and headed to the door.

"What?" she growled. "Where are you going?"

Smiling smugly, Jean-Claude pantomimed brushing his teeth before leaving the room.

Reut stared at the door, then at a spot on the floor, fidgeting in irritation. Finally, she managed to get herself up. *Okay, now what?* Ah, she had an idea! She walked over to her suitcase, undid the zipper of the small compartment, and pulled out a book. Then she picked up her phone from the desk and returned to bed. She knew Jean-Claude would take his time. His nighttime ritual went far beyond brushing his teeth: after swallowing a series of vitamins and obsessively tracking the status of his stubble, Jean-Claude preserved his face with a skin-care ritual no less fastidious than hers.

Her throat tightened. She wanted to get up and open the window but didn't have the energy. Adjusting her back against the headboard, she focused her eyes on the book, her hand hovering over the cover. Ah! She couldn't. She put the book down and looked at the wall. Her features hardened and scrunched, her eyebrows folding in on each other. Where the hell was Jean-Claude?! Why did he always have to take so long with his nightly grooming ceremony? She picked up her phone: nothing new, nothing new. A page of articles her smartphone recommended for her appeared. Reut clicked on the first link, read the headline, then returned to the recommendations page. Her finger scrolled down, down through the bottomless page. Impatient, she scrolled back up. Another glance at the screen. Another look at the door. Stalling, and down again. But, wait! That wasn't there before!—the third link—it must be a joke! She almost laughed, but her face went numb. Aliza Shor, her boring grad school friend, on her alerts page!

She clicked the link and found that it wasn't an article but a summary of an interview with Aliza from a literary television show, including a video clip. There was Aliza, walking in through a small door in a tasteless dress to join the interviewer. The audience clapped enthusiastically. Then she opened her mouth. She said something horribly predictable and laughed. Reut was convinced her laughter was fake, but the audience bought it. They echoed her and broke into another round of applause. Aliza continued speaking, and Reut—along with the audience—listened carefully. Her remarks seemed vapid, but all of a sudden, starting around the sixth sentence, Aliza's words came into focus, becoming more refined. A few sentences later, the clip ended. Oh, what was the point of that? She had to find the full interview and cast her verdict on Aliza! Then the door opened, making her jump. Jean-Claude was back.

While Reut, quick as a criminal, rushed to hide her phone, Jean-Claude closed the door behind him, announcing how tired he was. Reut watched him walk from the left window to the right, drawing the curtains. He then went to the writing desk and paused by the chair for a long time. Reut wanted to say something to him—nothing in particular, just something. But her discomfort deepened every moment he remained silent. Everything seemed strange and she couldn't say why.

Jean-Claude recommenced his pacing and walked toward the bed, pausing by the dresser this time.

As he undid his wide wristwatch, Reut said, "*Alors?*"

Jean-Claude placed his watch on the dresser, slowly looked up, then said back, "*Alors?*" in a tone tinged with surprise.

"Was it nice with everyone?"

"Where?" he said, taking a moment to understand. "Oh, very good."

Slipping into bed, Jean-Claude let out another yawn. As soon as his head met the pillow he jolted up and groped for the light switch, swatting Reut in the forehead. He turned it off.

"What are you doing?" she exclaimed.

"What—"

"Turn on the light please."

Jean-Claude obeyed. His gaze was fixed on a faraway point. Even in profile, Reut could see the defiant smile on his lips. Silence. Jean-Claude rolled his eyes, then said dryly, "*Bonne nuit.*"

Darkness.

Reut leapt up with the urge to slap Jean-Claude so hard that he would be incapable of smiling for an entire week. When her body hovered over his, all Reut did was click the light switch.

She barked, "What's with you?"

"What's with me?!"

"Yes, I—"

"What's with *me*?" he repeated, cutting her off. "Ha! Fantastic! What's with me." Jean-Claude sat up, ready to tell her everything on his mind, something he would have preferred to delay until after this vacation or, ideally, forever. "You, you are . . . " he began. "All night long, you—I don't know. Do I even have to say it? You know very well what I'm talking about."

"No, I am . . . " She meant to say something else, but all that left her mouth was, "What am I?"

Jean-Claude looked at her with annoyance and contempt. To himself, he mumbled, "*Dis-donc*, come on."

Reut stared at her husband, silently demanding an answer. Eventually, Jean-Claude deigned to elaborate. "I really—really—hoped it wouldn't be this way. But even here, you're—even here! You and your moods. That . . . miserable face, like something is always wrong. It's—I don't know. Really. Maybe you can tell me. Maybe I just don't understand. What's there not to be happy about here?! It's—no, actually, don't tell me—No, no, don't say a thing. It's going to drive me mad. What's wrong? What could possibly be wrong?"

Heatedly, Jean-Claude pushed off the blanket and turned

to get out of bed. One of his feet had just touched the floor when he turned back sharply. "Actually, do tell. Explain it to me. Why is everyone having fun down there and you just disappear! Tell me—what's so hard? Why can't you try, *for me*? Even here, you cause these scenes! You enjoy it, don't you? This is fun for you, is that it?"

Jean-Claude fell silent in his astonishment and pursed his lips. Reut also pushed off her blanket, sliding away from him.

Her measures proved unnecessary as Jean-Claude quietly and with doleful eyes continued, "I don't know. No, I don't know what to do. Do you understand you're making my life difficult, *chérie*? Why? I simply don't understand why you have to make things difficult. And when there is no reason for it! Don't you see, it's—Isn't it enough with the university, everything I have to go through now with that new idiot department chair, that imbecile! He wants to explain the procedures to me . . . How kind of him—don't you understand the difficulties I face? That everywhere I turn, people want something from me? That they're trying to—ah! I'm about to—"

Silence. The storm had returned. Hugging her knees nervously, Reut watched him. He seemed to be completely overcome with hatred. Then, all of a sudden, his fist slammed the dresser, a groan of frustration erupting from his throat. Reut recoiled.

"And you, of all people! I need you to be there for me, not to make my life even more difficult . . . Why can't you just be happy? For me? What's there not to be happy about?!"

Reut gathered herself to face his rhetorical question, but

remained still. Her fingers fluttered as she tried to corral her scattered, panicked thoughts. She was stunned: she couldn't remember the last time Jean-Claude revealed himself to her with such emotion, such accusation, such violence. And how could he make those baseless, cruel accusations, and in the middle of the night, no less, during this vacation he'd so been looking forward to! *He's* hurt? How dare he! What exactly was her crime?

She had not the faintest idea.

She finally spoke. "What are you talking about?! Weren't you at the trattoria tonight? You—are we talking about somebody else? Forget it. Really, it's—No, no, Jean-Claude, forget it. I understand everything. I thought that might be it, but I told myself I must be imagining it, that, or at least I hoped that wasn't it. Obviously I was wron—"

"*Mon dieu!*" he interjected. "Can you please speak clearly?!"

"You just can't stand to see me looking happy, that's what I'm talking about! It's—you just can't take it. Isn't that right?" She looked away from him, rebuking herself as *tipsha*, Hebrew for "stupid," several times. Then she got out of bed, hands clasped over her hips.

How to explain . . .

So many things ran through her mind. She didn't know where to begin. He understood nothing, had no clue what she wanted from him.

Finally, she began. "All night long, I entertain your friends, asking them questions, laughing at their jokes. Even your writer's creepy brother! Do you even—do you think I want that? Do you have any idea what kind of day I've had? Did you even ask? I've been up since seven o'clock this morning. And then that flight, which, by the way, I almost missed, and then that terrible train ride. You know I hate that!"

She fell silent and sat down on the edge of the bed. Then she huffed loudly, turning her head toward him. She couldn't decipher his expression. Was he angry? Did he agree with her? Perhaps he found this funny? His face was a blank canvas; anything painted on it would have seemed like reality to her.

Like a wounded animal, Reut crawled along the bed clumsily, drawing closer to Jean-Claude. She sat down beside him and said, defeated, "Can you tell me why we had to go to the restaurant in the first place? Why? Couldn't we have just come back here and let me rest? No. It always has to be your way. *Mon dieu!*—Do you have any idea how tired I am? Do you understand that, Jean-Claude? That I'm *drained*? That all I needed was just to sleep tonight, but for you—*for you!*—I said nothing, I tried to have fun, went out to that restaurant looking like hell. Entertained your friends. *Your* friends . . . Anything to not let you down . . . *Tipsha, tipsha!*" Mostly to herself, she added, "And here we are. Great. Fantastic! And now he scolds me about my face. Not happy? Did you even see me at dinner? Not happy. I never stopped talking!"

"I'm not talking about dinner."

"What?!" Reut roared. "I have no idea what you want from me!"

"*Bien.*"

"*Bien* what?"

Instead of answering, Jean-Claude desperately rubbed his temples, eyes shut. The massage hour had arrived, almost time to go to sleep. "We'll talk about it later," he finally said with a sigh.

In response to Reut's beseeching look, he elaborated. "Tomorrow. We'll talk about it tomorrow. Maybe . . . enough. I'm tired. Let's go to—"

"Now?!"

"Yes," Jean-Claude declared, turning the light back off.

But Reut was far from sleepy. She lay frozen in bed for nearly a full minute, her brain fuming in the void. She was so agitated, so alert—she couldn't sleep when things were left unresolved. She felt stifled. Her stomach ached. She felt an intensifying urge to shove a finger down her throat and make herself throw up. She wanted to get out of there. She didn't come all the way to Puglia for this awful punishment!

She'd leave right away. She'd walk out of Grigoryev's gorgeous summer home with her suitcase, which was fortunately still packed, and leave. Yes. That's what she'd do—but where exactly was the train station? And did the trains even run in the middle of the night? Probably not. *Tipsha*. She knew she was getting carried away, being ridiculous. But she couldn't take it anymore. Much worse than sharing a bed with a stranger was sharing a bed with a loved one who's become a stranger.

She had to get out of there. She couldn't breathe.

But the more Reut gave in to her runaway fantasy, the more palpably nauseated she became. She imagined

Jean-Claude's rebukes once he returned to Paris on his own, the endless catalog of accusations: *How dare you leave like that? You mortified me. You've lost your mind.*

No, Reut knew she couldn't leave right now. If she did, it would mean the end of her marriage. Everything would collapse at once. And what about Julian, their son, how would he handle all this? It would be too difficult. And their home, how would they—no, no. It was too complicated. She couldn't do it. She had to stay.

She got out of bed, hands on her hips. If she were at home she could have gone to the kitchen, made herself a cup of coffee, and sipped it slowly, in silence. Then she could have moved to the living room and fallen asleep on the couch. But, come to think of it, she never did that in their Paris home, and neither did Jean-Claude. They had simply carried on—two undeniable masters at avoiding confrontation.

And anyway, this wasn't her home. She was a guest. Finding the coffee, the right mug, an explanation if anyone happened to catch her in the act . . . no, it was impossible. Now this strange house made her feel even more stifled than the stranger snoring next to her.

Reut walked to the bathroom, lost in thought. Distractedly, she closed the door and sat on the toilet.

Ugh!

She stood back up immediately, wincing. Why did Jean-Claude never put down the toilet seat? Why was nothing easy for her? Always up, always up! God forbid the upright man delay his urges!

Reut lowered the seat and sat back down. A commendable stream rushed out for a few seconds, then, squeezing, she attempted to drain herself completely. But she had the disturbing feeling that something lingered. Her body refused full release.

Reut hurriedly washed her hands and returned to the bedroom, yet she still could not sleep. That was it! She'd wake him up, yes, she'd demand that he explain to her exactly what he'd meant. She'd demand that he listen to her as she explained exactly what she'd meant, too. This fight was so ridiculous, after all.

Approaching the bed with resolve, she restrained herself at the last moment. Attacking him now would only inspire a counterattack and she was much too shaken to endure that.

She was on the bed now. Six or seven seconds went by. She looked at him and said, "*Chéri.*" Shifting her body closer to his, she tried again. "*Chéri . . .*"

Silence.

"Jean-Claude, are you awake?"

An anguished glance at Jean-Claude's serene face. Another empty stare into space. It was pointless. Reut laid down and wrapped herself in the blanket. She breathed deeply into her diaphragm. And again. A sudden thought emerged: maybe this was for the best. Her previous thoughts were becoming all hazy and the exhaustion was overtaking her body.

Reut rested a hand on Jean-Claude's stomach and closed her eyes. She decided to let go of this madness that had seized her. Go to the train station *now*? In the middle of the night? Pick a fight with Jean-Claude on vacation at the writer's house? What was the big tragedy? She shouldn't have lost her temper and lashed out at him like that. And why did she lie to him? She had fun at the trattoria! Why did she say she was miserable? What would the next few days look like after this ridiculous fight?

She wanted to make up with him. Really make up. She wanted them to forget everything, starting tomorrow. More than that, she wanted tomorrow to herald a wonderful and intimate vacation. But tomorrow was intolerably far away— it had to be *now*. Yes! She'd get them to make up now, and they'd make love, and it would be thrilling, magnificent, and unforgettable!

She pushed her body against Jean-Claude's. He was still lying on his back, snoring delicately. She moved her hand from his stomach to his chest. Then she pushed up against him, one leg intertwined with his. Jean-Claude remained still. Reut began to move her hand in fluttering, circular movements, traveling between his chest, his neck, and his chin. Her breathing grew quicker, her genitals rubbing against the sheet. A few minutes passed, her desire grew, became a need. Then an intense snort spurted from Jean-Claude, as if Reut were a bothersome fly disrupting the sleeping horse.

Playfully, Reut ran her fingers from his chest to the ends of his boxer briefs, his hip bones and inner thighs. Her breathing was heavy. Lips fluttering on his shoulder, kissing slowly, a shy tongue emerging on occasion. She hoisted herself onto her knees. Her hand kept rubbing his lower belly as her lips moved to his neck and chest.

A grunt. At last! A potential sign of awakening!

Reut was spurred on, kissing him faster, wetter, slipping a hand down his boxers.

A slight hardening, a reasonable start. Her fingers brushed the sides delicately, then, in a flash her entire hand wrapped around it, sliding and releasing it with passion.

Pulling away her hand. Applying spit. Returning, regripping. Lightly sliding her hand from the tip down and back up again.

A pause.

Reut looked at Jean-Claude, trying to gauge how awake he was. It was impossible for him to still be asleep—she felt his body, his quickening breaths, his thickening member. Then why didn't he say anything? Why didn't he try to touch her? Reut needed his warmth. She needed to feel the two of them together, synchronized. He couldn't stay this way, on his back like an ironing board!

She pushed down his boxer briefs for a little more freedom of movement: a grunt of confirmation from Jean-Claude. Then, another—of encouragement this time—of anticipation for the touch of her tongue.

Reut bowed her head slowly, resetting her body. Her lower back started to hurt. A little kiss to the tip, a kiss to the base, and another, and another—more drawn out. But he didn't harden. Where were the days when he rose promptly to meet her?

Stroking the sad penis, Reut was flooded with a wave of irritation. No doubt Jean-Claude was awake; why was he letting her carry on if he didn't want her? Why the hell didn't he move?

Sharply, Reut lifted her head. Her lust had dried out. She recalled suddenly that before their stupid fight she'd planned to get up early to do some reading before breakfast. But just as she was about to lay back down, a tense hand stopped her head, pushing it gently downward, back to him. Another grunt from Jean-Claude, and then, for the first time since she'd started—words!

"Please," he murmured, "keep going."

And so she did. Her back hurt and her jaw hurt, but she kept going. She couldn't stop now, after everything she'd already invested in this scene.

Her perseverance paid off: within two minutes of patient monotony, she had achieved the hope of a more stable erection. But three minutes later, there was still so much work ahead of her.

Enough! She was worn out. Reut wanted to make Jean-Claude happy, to please him, to reconcile. But not like this, without any reciprocation or communication!

"Jean-Claude, I—" she muttered, lying down. "I'm sorry, it's . . . *bonne nuit.*"

Reut didn't wait for a reply. She felt exhausted and ridiculous. Sad. She curled into the fetal position, swept herself toward the right side of the bed, back turned to Jean-Claude.

After a short while, a relaxed sensation arose within her, deepening her breaths—long inhales through the mouth to begin, then smaller, more discreet breaths through the nose. At this point, Reut could tell from the fog descending on her that she was finally falling asleep. The storyline of a dream was unspooling, the set rearranging, the protagonists introduced in her mind. But then all of a sudden she became aware of their ephemerality, and they vanished within her.

Reut shrunk further into herself, focusing on her breath, exhaling distraction. She'd be prepared for the next scene change, ready to be carried away by whatever new characters appeared before her.

But just then a hand was placed upon her shoulder.

The rustle of a shifting body.

And wonder of wonders: he moved! The ironing board had come alive!

Curling up beside Reut, Jean-Claude wrapped his body around hers. His touch was so soothing: her back tight against his stomach, his heavy breathing against her skin, his legs bound up with hers, his arm embracing her. That was all she needed, actually. The sensation of him close to her, the impression that he longed for her too, that they were making a mutual effort. She knew that Jean-Claude needed to lay flat as a board to fall asleep. If he turned in her direction now, that meant he was *choosing* her intimacy. Perhaps he wished to reconcile, too?

A poke.

A poke in her lower back. What once was only half-hard was now as erect as it could get. Before she could think to respond, she felt Jean-Claude's hand crawling under her shirt, grabbing one of her breasts. An aggressive grab.

And another poke, and another. The space resounded with Jean-Claude's groans as he rubbed against Reut, squeezing her breasts.

But she was too tired to follow through. Why did he suddenly wake up? How did he get hard? It had seemed so impossible before!

And then she felt a finger force its way inside her, spreading her open, demanding freedom of movement. But she was entirely unprepared! She was wiped out, dry, and there had been no foreplay to speak of. He hurt her. She tried to push his hand away, to tell him "enough," but he wrapped his other hand around her body and she felt paralyzed. Then—he penetrated. The finger had fulfilled its purpose. He dove straight into the heart of a desert. Another thrust, and another, diving deep, as if there were some oasis inside her he was thrusting to find.

Reut let him keep going. He was already there, he had already hurt her, what difference did it make now? At any rate, she knew it was only a matter of minutes. She was very familiar with the mumbling that emerged from his mouth: a lot of "*ah-oui*" and a little "*putain.*" And yes, he was finished in less than a minute.

"*Je t'aime,*" he exhaled, maintaining his tradition of pecking the back of her neck.

For a few more moments, breathing heavily against her, he held her. Then, turning onto his back again—he fell asleep.

THE FIRST MORNING

REUT woke up at four minutes after seven. She had barely slept, and the night had included an urgent trip to the bathroom, a mosquito invasion, and a succession of anxiety dreams. She returned to wakefulness with a sense of unease. She felt she'd left the last dream at its climax, after its inner logic had been established, no longer requiring her presence in order to run its course.

She was back in Paris, she remembered that much for sure. She was making an important phone call while waiting for a transfer on the Metro. During the conversation, she experienced a bout of agoraphobia: the people around her nearly trampled her, and she could barely hear the person on the other end of the line. She repeated herself over and over again, shouting. A couple on the train was kissing passionately, the man fondling the woman's body in front of everyone. The woman was enjoying it. A short guy walked by with a device that emitted the electronic sounds of French *chansons*. Someone bumped into her shoulder. She was yelling. She had something important to say! Then all of sudden she woke up, staring blankly at the wall. It took her a moment to recall that she was in Puglia, not at home.

She slipped out of bed, sneaking a look at Jean-Claude, still sound asleep. After yawning twice in a row she walked over to the bathroom, where she brushed her teeth more slowly than usual, scrubbing her molars. Then she turned on the faucet, arched her back so she could stick her face in the stream of water, and remained that way for thirty seconds, unable or unwilling to pull herself away. On her way downstairs everything looked new and unfamiliar. She was surprised to find how flawed her memories from the previous night had been. The house was much larger and more impressive than she'd thought. Impressive not necessarily because of its size, but rather because of its unique appearance, its soothing color palette, and the collection of eclectic knickknacks.

Coming down the wide, wooden staircase, Reut noticed the paintings on the walls—lots of portraits, mostly morose; a few landscapes in the same style as the one in her bedroom—and on the second floor, some walls painted a pink beige, others constructed from rows of massive golden-brown bricks. Reut loved the warmth they emanated and the way they complemented the Moorish ceiling design and the cheerful floor tile pattern: intertwined diamonds and flowers in shades of turquoise, yellow, green, and burgundy.

But more than anything else in the house, Reut loved the kitchen. From the colorful dishes to the sleek dining table with a retro touch, from the burgeoning spice collection to the red crockery hanging on the wall, from the enormous windows to the exotic plants, from the bamboo bar to the tall statues—everything was to her taste.

Soft morning light. An unfamiliar view outside the gorgeous kitchen windows. Reut stretched her body with pleasure, up, up, up, then right and left. That unhappy night with Jean-Claude and her broken sleep now seemed miles away. Meaningless. She was alone now, totally alone, no rustling within or without. A rare moment.

Amid the silence, she walked leisurely over to the cabinets searching for coffee. After a determined round of opening and closing doors—another hope, another disappointment—her idyllic morning faded away: there was no coffee maker she knew how to use. Only a stovetop espresso pot.

"*Bien*," she said out loud, assuming that someone who knew how to work the coffee maker would wake up soon. This idea was comforting and upsetting in equal measures: her moments of solitude were numbered.

Reut sat at the bar table with a glass of lemonade, an open book, and a pen. To her joy, she was able to read her research book for more than fifteen minutes without interruption. But then she was pulled back into reality.

"*Salut*!"

It took Reut a moment to spot the source of the voice. She straightened herself frantically, and before she had a chance to answer Bernard, she found him bare-chested just inches away from her. The kiss-kiss ritual. Reut had never gotten used to performing this ritual on vacation. What was the point, when sharing a home, of repeating this greeting every morning? The tradition epitomized the vast abyss between the Israeli and French mentalities. The greeting rules that had been taught to her since childhood were often breached and entirely mood-dependent: a wave, a kiss, a warm hug, an indifferent smile, or nothing at all.

"You're an early riser," Bernard commented cheerfully, walking over to the counter. "*C'est bien, c'est bien . . .*"

Reut noticed his accent for the first time this morning. Southern, no doubt. The off-kilter way he pronounced the word "*bien*" was a dead giveaway. She wanted to share her insight, perhaps tell him how much she loved Montpellier, but all she ended up saying was, "I suppose I am." She watched with curiosity as he took a glass from the cabinet, placed it on the counter, then got a bottle of cold water from the fridge and poured it. He downed the water in a single gulp, sighed with loud satisfaction, then turned sharply toward Reut.

"Would you like some?"

"No, it's—I have some lemonade. *Merciii.*"

"*D'accord.*"

Reut felt uncomfortable, judging herself for the clumsy way she'd spoken. Maybe the prolonged solitude she'd enjoyed that morning had been enough to make her forget how to communicate with others. Or perhaps it was Bernard's chiseled, tan, and unbearably bare body that had discombobulated her. He was wearing nothing but tight bicycle shorts, and was glistening with sweat that had yet to evaporate from his perfectly muscular torso—a geometry more impressive than Reut would ever expect on a body well into its fifth decade. He told her he'd just returned from his morning run: ninety minutes up one of the mountains overlooking the sea. He would take her there sometime in the next few days, he said.

The exterior Reut listened to Bernard. But the one on the inside, the tense one, didn't know how to behave in front of his nudity, and she would have preferred he cover himself rather than force it on her. It took too much mental effort, a heightened awareness. She was worried he might notice her noticing his body, or worse—marveling at its beauty. To Bernard, going shirtless must have been mindless, like a child scampering about on a sunny day. A man naked in public was not sexually objectified. He was just a man at ease. And yet, no matter how attractive the torso before her, Reut was uncomfortable talking to naked strangers. As she spoke to Bernard, she persistently policed her gaze, training it on his eyes. She thought Bernard took her focus as a compliment.

The sound emitted by the espresso maker invited Bernard to take a seat. Their exchange was pleasant, though brief: after draining his second cup of coffee, Bernard rose and said he was going to shower. He asked Reut to excuse him and added, a mischievous smile on his face, that he'd be seeing her again soon.

After he left, Reut spent a few idle moments staring at the bamboo bar, her fingers mindlessly peeling the skin of her lips. Then she opened her book again, taking hold of the pen. She scanned the first page, then shut the book and grabbed the coffeepot, pointing the spout toward her cup. A few final drops slid out. Reut smiled playfully and got up, satisfyingly arching her back.

She moved toward the windows and took in the view for a while. But all at once, the idyll collapsed. How could this have happened to her? And with *him*, of all people! She was mortified. Out of everyone, it was the handsome runner who was forced to look upon this ghastly sight—this aging, wrinkled, ghost face deprived of sleep and concealer. Reut rushed out of the kitchen before anyone else arrived, climbing swiftly up the stairs. Panting lightly, she opened the bedroom door, pulled her toiletry kit out of her suitcase, and glanced at Jean-Claude on her way out: he was still in bed, sleeping off his hangover.

At the bathroom mirror: damage control. A base layer of makeup. She sighed with satisfaction. Now she could bear to look at herself. As she allowed the spackle a few moments to absorb properly, she began lining her eyes. While she dedicated her attention to her right eye, someone jiggled the doorknob aggressively once, then twice. On the other side of the door, a surprised voice asked, "What's this? What—"

"One moment! I'll be right—"

"Tutu, is that you in there?"

"I'm coming, Jean-Claude! Ah, just wait a second. Coming, coming."

Reut opened the door. Wordlessly, Jean-Claude gave her arm a quick rub as he nearly ran to the toilet. A rumbling stream of urine coupled with a sigh of relief sounded as Reut left the room.

Wandering through the house, she thought she heard people in the kitchen, was convinced she recognized Bernard and Mikhail. They were speaking loudly, sounding a bit on edge. She began to backtrack toward the living room. But then, a few steps away, she turned on her heels again, back to the kitchen. What was she supposed to do in the living room? Sit around like an idiot? She was hungry and wanted some food. Reut hated being robbed of her basic freedom of movement in other people's homes.

Gently pressing the doorknob, she hesitantly opened the kitchen door. She heard Bernard saying, "—ould try in, in the part of—"

Bernard fell silent when he heard the door, and Reut closed it with a start, muttering a soft "*pardon.*" In that brief moment, she had spotted Mikhail and Marion sitting at the table with Bernard. Their postures implied a private conversation. But even if this were the case, why did she have to leave like that? Frozen awkwardly outside the door, she didn't know what to do next. She felt hollow with hunger.

But just as she was about to return to the living room, Mikhail called out to her. "Reut, *chérie*, come in."

As she walked obediently back into the kitchen, he continued, "Come, sit with us. Would you like something to dri—"

"Where'd you run off to?" Bernard interrupted. "We're just settling a work matter. Even here we talk shop. You must have heard of Mazzarini? About the movie he's making based on Mikhail's book?"

"Oh, yes," Reut replied, kissing Marion hello. As she moved on to Mikhail's cheeks, Bernard elaborated, "Well, we're having a few disagreements about the music. What we want it to sound like in certain segments. So we were just talking abou—"

"He's the film's music producer," Marion interjected, her fingers grazing Reut's hand to get her attention. Then, she moved her hand over to Bernard's arm. "Why are you being so vague? It's impossible to understand you like that, sweetie. You should start by saying you're the film's musical producer. Otherwise how is she supposed to—"

"Yes, *chérie*, you're right." Bernard gave Marion's cheek a peck. At the prompting of her fingers pressing into his arm, he turned his face toward her and gave her lips a quick kiss, then another, more sensual one.

"So," Bernard returned his gaze to Reut, "what I was going to say. . . I really am indecipherable today! Forgive me, Reut, I'm truly unbearable. My brain doesn't function properly when I'm hungry."

Bernard rose quickly, returning to Marion's lips for one final kiss, then announced he would be getting breakfast started.

Walking over to the stove, Mikhail mumbled indulgently, "You really are unbearable."

The group moved at vacation pace: about ten minutes passed before Jean-Claude joined them and twenty more minutes before Katya appeared—a long enough gap for the men to bring up the familiar stereotype: "Ha-ha, these women! Why does it take them so long to get ready?"

The two latecomers joined in the breakfast preparation. There was certainly an abundance of work to be done: Bernard took on crêpe duty; Mikhail's job was to slice focaccia and cheese, then squeeze oranges for juice; Marion took charge of the fruit salad; Reut—vegetable salad; standing beside Bernard, Jean-Claude manned the omelet station; Katya, who showed up at just the right moment, took it upon herself to set the table. Only Pavel was missing. "We won't wait for him," Mikhail averred. "He's likely to sleep in till noon."

The first few minutes of eating were peaceable: sporadic praise for the food, an accolade for the quality of the cheese and the focaccia, repeated requests to pass this or that item. Everyone was at ease, comfortable just being in their own skins and partaking of the bounty on the table. Reut liked this dynamic, so unique to vacations—the way a prolonged stay with a small group of people reframes and refreshes the intensity of conversations. The feeling that it is allowed, even appropriate, to refrain from constant talk.

When they reached the leisurely snacking phase—when everyone's hunger had already been satiated and eating continued for the sake of gourmandise or boredom—the conversation started ramping back up, flowing toward the same topic that occupied vacationers' minds each morning: What should they do today?

Mikhail and Marion were members of the conservative camp ("Let's go back to yesterday's beach") and Jean-Claude and Katya were liberals ("Let's find a new beach"). Bernard formed a one-man anarchist party ("Anything goes") while

Reut started a radical subsect ("Why don't we go sightseeing instead of going to the beach?")

Reut, who'd grown up in Herzliya, by the sea, wasn't easily enticed by the nearby beaches—at least not as easily as her European counterparts. When she was younger she enjoyed a light jog along the boardwalk. Always active, then. Lying on the sand seemed to her awfully dull. The little research she had done on Puglia offered up several destinations she much preferred to the beach: there was Lecce, the sixth-largest city in the region, filled with Baroque architecture, and nicknamed by the proud locals "Florence of the South," or Ostuni, known as the "White City," which was about two hundred meters above sea level and had a Greek feel. People had admired its beauty even back in the Stone Age. Reut also hoped to visit Alberobello, with its famous fourteenth-century trulli houses, or the Otranto Cathedral, famous for its stunning mosaics and the skulls of the saints.

Not wanting to be too pushy, Reut mentioned only Lecce and Ostuni. She casually brought them up as options, emphasizing that it was just a suggestion. But as the words left her mouth, an intense desire arose in her to see one of those sites that very day, despite her poor sleep the previous night. She knew most of them wanted to go to the beach, but she ached to be in motion—to get to know Puglia, to stumble upon its treasures, to let her feet carry her rather than obey maps or the whims of others. How would she tell the group that she would actually love for them to go to the beach without her? She'd only joined them the previous night, a latecomer! How hard could she tug on the social fabric before it unraveled?

"No," Mikhail determined. "Today isn't good for Lecce. Lecce is beautiful. *Vot.* But we need to plan ahead, to leave early. If we took the train from here, if I'm not mistaken, it would be—"

"*Chérie*, it's too late today," Jean-Clause interrupted. "We could try tomorrow, maybe. Or, actually no! Didn't we want to go to Otranto first? To see the cathedral?"

"Sure," Reut replied. "I'd like to see that, too. So we could go to Otranto tomorrow. Perhaps we should—"

"Did you say *Ostuni*?" Bernard exclaimed. "If you want, we could go there today. There's a shop there I'd like to visit. Come—we'll go there. Ostuni is not too far."

"Ooh!" Marion raised her eyebrows. "What kind of shop?"

"Nothing that would interest you, *chouchou*. I don't know if you could call it a shop, really. It's—Mikhail, you know what I'm talking about. Vincenzo's place . . ."

"Ah, Vincenzo! Of course. Fabulous, bring back some good things."

"And who is this Vincenzo?" Marion continued her line of questioning.

"An old guy," Bernard said. "He sells olive oil made by his family out of his home, along with some local wine and pantry products. The last time I was here I really went wild. After I visited him, I had to buy a second suitcase for everything I'd bought! How much was it, Mikhail? Six, maybe seven bottles of olive oil? You know that the best olive oil in Puglia is made in Ostuni—"

"Wonderful!" Reut cried with excitement, cutting him off.

"*Bien,*" Bernard said, slamming his fist on the table. "So we'll go? Yes, we'd better go today. That way, if we decide to have dinner at home one night, we'll have some tasty treats."

"I . . ." Marion murmured bitterly. "But . . . today?!"

Sighing playfully, Bernard rose slowly from his chair and walked over to Marion. Massaging her shoulders—long, strong squeezes—he said, "Come on, *chérie*, is there any day when you *would* want to go? I know you. You'd be dying to come back here after one hour in Ostuni. It's fine, go to the beach with them. Have fun. I'll see you tonight. All right? *Ça va, mon amour?*"

Marion turned her head back, looking up with a mixture of sadness and reproach. After she pursed her lips for a kiss and Bernard obliged, she said, "*D'accord.*" A brief pause. "But don't come back too late."

Reut carelessly rolled her eyes. She felt uncomfortable, witnessing Marion's manipulation of Bernard. She couldn't bear the tyrannical mellifluousness of Marion's voice, that elegant mask she wore in order to control Bernard. But Bernard knew he was being possessed, and he liked it, there was no doubt about that. Perhaps that's what made watching the two in action so disconcerting.

Reut had often come across women of Marion's breed. How she loathed them. And how, at times, she wished she was more like them. Reut had suspected Marion's nature the moment they'd first met in the foyer the previous night. That morning, as they discussed Mazzarini, she was almost sure of it, and now she was convinced: Marion was a bossy seductress, the kind who used her artificial sweetness to castrate both men and women.

Because Marion's manipulations were not directed solely at Bernard. And Reut was in no way oblivious to the ones cast in her direction: the hand that, as if by chance, touched hers—caressing, condescending; the saccharine looks Marion gave her after kissing Bernard. These were brief glances, supposedly innocent, but Reut gleaned their true meaning: boundary setting. Reut must not make too much eye contact with Bernard, lest Marion feel threatened.

Reut wasn't concerned that Jean-Claude would feel threatened by Bernard or any other man. Sometimes she even wished for the opportunity for another man to spark Jean-Claude's possessive urge, make him feel the ground falling out from beneath him, if only for a moment. Enough with that nonchalant self-confidence and his faith in good old Reut sticking around! Jean-Claude was so self-assured that not only did he not suffer from jealousy, but she suspected he also took pleasure in watching her interact with his male friends. As if their innocent flirtations with her were, in fact, flirtations with him—a pat on his ego, a game of affirmation, a testament to their true friendship.

Indeed, Jean-Claude saw no problem with Bernard inviting Reut to join him in Ostuni. On the contrary—let them go and get acquainted. Reut was his special envoy in his mission to strengthen his relationship with Bernard. Either way, Jean-Claude preferred to spend his day relaxing at the beach. All of the alcohol he'd consumed the previous night had left its mark. He felt tired and weak, and this concerned him. Besides that, he was still upset with Reut. For not understanding him, for denying his allegations. A little distance between them, coupled with the sea breeze, might alleviate his bitterness.

THE WHITE CITY

BERNARD and Reut were ready to hit the road a few minutes after noon. To reach this point, Reut had already needed a thorough bathing, two outfit changes, and makeup touch-ups. She had taken a longer than usual shower because of that burning sensation she'd felt that morning when she peed, and—worse yet—later, when she was sitting in the kitchen. But Reut couldn't afford to be unwell—not when embarking on an excursion, and certainly not with Bernard.

The thought of spending an entire day in Ostuni with Bernard made Reut simultaneously nervous and giddy. She still hadn't formed a firm opinion of him. Sometimes, he seemed like just another one of Jean-Claude's Parisian intellectual sheep. But other times he appeared intriguing, attractive, and unexpected. At any rate, she was curious about him, no doubt about that. She also wanted him to find her attractive, there was no doubt about that, either. The only remaining question was why.

Bernard in no way represented Reut's taste in men. On the surface, he appeared too frivolous, too successful, too athletic. A fun-lover, a womanizer, carefree. A man who, unlike Jean-Claude, didn't require a gaggle of friends to feel happy, because his love of life was deeply rooted in his soul. Reut had never been with a man like that, for fear that he would bore her, misunderstand her, or—worse—lead her to judge herself for her lack of inner joy.

The outfit she finally settled on: an airy white cotton shirt with a wide, square neckline that revealed her freckled shoulders. She'd debated for a while, then finally opted for a bottle green stretchy skirt that came down just above her knees. It had been a long time since Reut had last worn it. In recent years it had begun to seem too tight, not age appropriate. But, wonder of wonders, the skirt had made its way into her suitcase along with the question: Why not?

Reut and Bernard headed out while everyone else was in their rooms. Pavel had only just woken up, which spurred the beachgoers to get organized. As they walked to the train station, Reut brought up Pavel as an icebreaker. She asked Bernard if he had any idea why Pavel had slept in so late. Did something happen to him the previous night?

"No, of course not," Bernard said calmly. "It's been . . . he's always been this way."

"What way?"

"In bed, until late." Bernard pondered in silence, then added: "He's . . . he's been like this at least the last few times I've seen him here."

"How long have you known him?"

"Pavel's been coming every summer since Mikhail bought the Puglia house."

They were quiet for a few moments. Bernard walked quickly, wearing an owl-like expression as he looked around him inquisitively.

Shyly, Reut asked, "And Mikhail? You two seem to have known each other a long time . . . "

"Mikhail is, well, like family. We've known each other for years."

"How nice," Reut mumbled, smiled, and went quiet again. She had many other, more invasive questions for Bernard, but she sensed this wasn't the right time. Bernard had answered her graciously, no doubt, but she suspected he barely even noticed her, being far more interested in the hustle and bustle of the alleyways. Perhaps when they reached Ostuni she'd have a chance to ask all of her questions—assuming, of course, that the two of them would form a rapport, that she would loosen up. At this early stage of the day, Reut half hoped and half doubted this would happen.

It was almost two o'clock when they stepped off the train. Reut was surprised by how quickly the journey had gone by: no wait at the station, and then no more than a thirty-minute ride, such a blessed contrast to the previous day. As they walked out of the station in Ostuni, she barely even noticed the wondrous place where they'd arrived; all she could see was Bernard's face.

As they walked, Reut maintained eye contact as he told her more about Mazzarini's film. Back on the train, she had asked a casual question about it, expecting a perfunctory response. Nothing had prepared her for the eager, revealing answer he offered.

Bernard laid out, in great detail, his many dilemmas about the music he was composing and producing for the film. Unfurling the ideas he had innovated and the risks they involved, he sounded like an excitable boy: associative, clumsy at times, jumping wildly from one topic to the next.

The previous night, at the trattoria, Mikhail had described Bernard as "one of the most gifted cellists in the world today," in addition to being a "celebrated super-producer." He added that Bernard had been born to a wealthy family, and didn't work for the money. "Everything he does," Mikhail concluded, "is for the sake of art." And now this artist, this super-producer, was walking beside her, sharing with her—Reut—his plans, his many quandaries and concerns, as if he were a mere intern just starting out in his career. And another surprise: unlike Jean-Claude, who voiced his conundrums but always answered himself, Bernard seemed to actually want her opinion.

This discussion was only the appetizer for an entire day of long walks and engrossing conversations. A strange day for Reut. There was no better word to describe the time she spent with Bernard. Everything else she felt during those hours— excitement, joy, insecurity, and sorrow—all distilled into that feeling of stifling strangeness. A combination of euphoria and grief.

Her grief was overwhelming and entirely inexplicable: Who or what was she losing? Who was Bernard? Why should she care about him? What did she even know about him?

And therein, perhaps, lay the heart of the strangeness: Reut felt that she knew quite a bit about him. And yet nothing at all.

From the moment they stepped off the train until their return to Polignano a Mare, Reut became Bernard's acquaintance, his fan, his good friend, and his partner—at moments even his wife. She was all of these people in spirit, not always noticing when and how. The day was marvelously long and overflowing with different moods, moments of every variety.

Their meeting with Vincenzo took on special status in Reut's mind, serving as an important turning point. They arrived at his home after wandering the city for about an hour. Bernard would have liked to arrive later because he planned to make a hefty purchase, but he determined that they shouldn't risk it: "Vincenzo likes to wander around and he never picks up his phone."

They were greeted at the door by Angela, Vincenzo's wife, a large, smiling woman in her sixties. She told them that Vincenzo was, predictably, on one of his walks, and would be back soon. The visitors did not have much choice but to oblige when Angela pleaded, "Make yourselves at home!"

She was in the middle of preparing a stunning meal, working with a bounty of ingredients whose final purpose Reut could not predict.

"What, what's all—" Reut murmured, suddenly remembering she ought to address Angela in English. "What is all this for?"

Angela's English, however, could be summed up with two

words: "I'm sorry." In the Apulian dialect she added, "What's that, sweetheart? I can't understand."

"She, *ella*," Bernard started, then decided to translate Reut's words into Spanish, which he had a stronger grasp of: "*Ella pregunta por que todos estos platos.*"

Bernard knew from his previous visits that his passable Spanish and Angela's broken Spanish would allow them to understand each other well enough. She told him that the entire family was coming to their home that night—a birthday celebration for her "beloved *nipote*," Michele, the sixth of her eight grandchildren.

Moved by this magical place she'd discovered, Reut examined Angela and Bernard as they conversed: sitting tall, Bernard took occasional sips of the lemonade Angela had poured them, appearing happy and relaxed. Angela scampered about the kitchen as she called out to him, looking like an orchestra conductor who could see the entire score of the meal but knew which part needed her attention at any given moment.

Every few minutes, she extracted a little taste of the appetizers for them to sample—a bit of friselle, an Apulian bread with tomatoes and pine nuts, a spoonful of mashed fava, a bite of polpette or baked eggplants. Reut accepted each bite she was offered. She remembered Jean-Claude's plea: "When southern Italians offer you food, you must always say yes! Otherwise, they take it as an insult."

And yet, when Vincenzo finally arrived, the southern eating habits became much more challenging for Reut. Not only did Vincenzo's return signal the uncorking of a fabulous bottle of wine (compliments of the family vineyard), but also the introduction of an abundance of local cheeses and meats he'd just acquired from a friend. Vincenzo served these delicacies on the table in the yard, by order of his wife. Now that he was home, she allowed herself to demand to be left alone: "*Se nó ngi fazz attimb*!" she warned him. "Or else I'll never finish in time!"

Vincenzo was elated to see Bernard again after several years. He patted Bernard many times on his back and arms, spoke vigorously, and filled the air with incessant, rumbling laughter. His hands were almost always on the move: slicing sliver after sliver of salami and cheese. When his hands weren't busy handling the food, they were on the wine bottle. He consistently refilled his guests' glasses before they were anywhere close to empty.

Vincenzo wasn't able to communicate with Reut. Like Angela, his English was basic at best. And yet their language barrier did not prevent him from sharing his enthusiasm for her presence, for having honored him with her "beautiful" company. "*Bella*," he repeated as he poured her more wine; *bella* as he placed another piece of cheese or meat on her plate without being asked; *bella* as he watched her, a beaming smile on his face, then said something in Spanish to Bernard that she couldn't understand. The third time this happened, Reut demanded that Bernard translate for her.

"He . . . " Bernard smiled mischievously and sipped on his wine. "He says that my, my wife, is very charming. I told him you aren't . . . ha-ha, as far as he's concerned, you're my wife!" He quickly picked up his glass, signaled to the others to join him, and then, his voice rising, declared, "Cheers! *Salute*!"

Reut left Vincenzo and Angela's house very tipsy. Thanks to Vincenzo, who'd made sure to keep her glass full, she was always under the false impression that she was still on her first round. A complete lack of control: true pleasure.

She was so baffled by how much fun she was having that she laughed constantly, despite understanding almost nothing of the conversation. On second thought, perhaps this wasn't such a mystery after all. Intimacy needed no language. If anything, language served as an accompaniment to intimacy only once it has already been established.

That's exactly how it felt with Vincenzo and Angela: something about their sincere smiles, their warm eyes, their energetic way of addressing her and each other, their voices free of any artifice—these all formed an instant intimacy. She felt at home, as if she and Bernard had visited them dozens of times before. As if it were their spot.

They said goodbye to Vincenzo and Angela and left, Bernard carrying two large tote bags, and Reut carrying a third. Some of the gifts Vincenzo had insisted on giving her, such as the basil pesto and the *orecchiette*, she chose to slip into her purse. Bernard's bags also contained small gifts: some jams and savory spreads, a package of handmade pasta. Then there were the many bottles he'd purchased:

two primitivo wines from Vincenzo's family vineyard, a special digestif they had just started producing, two slender bottles of extra virgin olive oil, and three vials of balsamic oil—a classic made with negroamaro and malvasia nera grapes, and two bolder flavors, one saffron and orange, the other apple.

"There's really nothing here you could go without," Reut insisted, giggling under the influence of the grapes. "It's like with shoes: every bottle has its own special purpose!"

Laden down, Reut and Bernard headed back into the city. It was already 5:30 p.m., and yet there was no sign of evening on the street: the sun was generous, the people pleasantly clamoring. Reut couldn't say exactly what had happened during their wandering. Later, she remembered bumping into something that hurt, but the pain had soon lifted. She recalled talking a lot about things she saw—here's a pretty building, there's a curious character, and here's another enchanting corner. She kept wanting to share her thoughts with Bernard. She wanted to talk constantly, yet couldn't, interrupted by intoxicated bursts of laughter that erupted from her throat.

Then, all of a sudden, Marion called. And how joyfully he answered her call! He was so glad to hear *chouchou*'s voice. Stepping away for privacy, Bernard left Reut alone. A few moments' wait, impatience, sauntering over to some nearby stone steps, sitting down. But she couldn't be bothered to sit for long. She stood up and looked around. Where was she? How did they even get there? She had no idea.

The beauty of the place evoked a sense of awe, as she stood on a step that was the first in a twisting cascade spilling onto a small, square piazza. The piazza, flanked on two sides by old houses, left a narrow horizon from which she could see the sea and one of the city's steep alleys. The piazza itself was on a slight incline, constructed in tiers. Ostuni itself was an infinite series of ups and downs.

Each level of the piazza revealed new details and different colors: small iron balconies hung from every house, draped with domesticated and wild plants; long string lights stretched from side to side and would, at nightfall, shed soft light over the café's outdoor tables, shaded by elegant golden parasols, and one rebellious, burgundy parasol. Reut marveled at the way these colors all blended together against the uneven white backdrop of houses. In spite of its nickname, "the white city," this town was not entirely white. At times it was gray, even an orange-pink, when the walls of houses chose to revolt.

But somehow, and perhaps this was the secret of the city's charm, in spite of these many other colors, it was the blinding light against all the white that caught her eye.

Reut walked down the steps, hoping to find a sign that would signal her location. Too impatient to look around carefully, she walked into a gelato shop and asked the woman behind the counter for the name of the piazza. But the name slipped from her agitated mind as soon as it was spoken. At any rate, facing the cashier, she had found more important matters to occupy her mind: picking flavors of gelato and deciding whether to enjoy them in a cup or a cone.

Carrying a cone laden with scoops of pistachio and dark chocolate, Reut walked out of the shop when suddenly—a startled jump! Her bag of purchases from Vincenzo. Where was it?! She hurried up the steps and spent a few tense moments searching for the bag. Didn't she leave it on the top step?! Then she spent a few more seconds looking around for Bernard. He was no longer in the same spot where he'd walked over to talk to Marion. Her ice cream started to melt. A feeling of helplessness. And her cellphone! Where was that? Did she also—no. Her phone was still right there, in her bag. She took four large licks of gelato, taming it before it lost all control, then clumsily opened her bag to call Bernard when, all of a sudden, a surprised voice called out to her: "You're here!"

"Yes!" she cried out.

She made a half-turn and finally spotted Bernard: he was climbing up the steps from the enchanting piazza. Reut watched him with concealed discomfort, confused by the way he had used the formal *vous* with her. They'd spent an entire day together, calling each other *tu*, and now, with a single word, it had all unraveled.

"I've been looking for you. Where were you?"

"I . . ."

"You left your tote bag here. I've got it."

"Ah, good. *Merciii* . . ."

Reut fell silent. She didn't know what had taken hold of her: nothing she said came out the way she'd meant it, everything getting twisted as it left her mouth. She watched herself as if from above, struggling to talk, a five-year-old girl hold-ing a melting ice cream cone. She felt she'd had too much to drink, that she'd messed up, that she was being scolded—a sensation Reut was highly familiar with, and which didn't diminish with age. But then Bernard offered his charming movie star smile, and everything was all right again, as it had, in fact, been all along. She thought he seemed quite amused with her. He asked if she wanted him to hold her gelato.

"Oh, I forgot!" she cried. "I wanted to get you one, too."

"That's all right," he said. "Come, let's find somewhere to sit for a bit and then we'll start heading back. It's getting late."

"Marion . . . ? Does she want you to—"

"I spoke to her. They're still at the beach. We'll meet them there and have a drink."

"*D'accord.*"

A brief pause to think.

"Maybe I should also call Jean-Cla—"

As she spoke, Reut made a hasty move toward her bag. The ice cream cone slipped out of her hand and dove quickly, crashing against the pavement.

THE SECOND NIGHT

BERNARD told Marion they would be back around 8:30 p.m., but Marion still called at eight o'clock to ask where they were. Bernard replied that they would return soon, but "soon" became delayed, leading to quite a few more calls and text messages. Jean-Claude also called Reut once, around 9:30. Reut didn't pick up and quickly silenced her phone. She was enjoying herself too much, fearing that any beep might break the spell of her conversation with Bernard.

They were sitting at a fabulous restaurant recommended by a local couple they'd chatted with during their aperitivo. According to the original plan, they were supposed to leave Ostuni after having drinks, but then came the nice couple's recommendation—or, more accurately, their plea—along with a sense of freedom and wholesome hunger (which Reut did not take for granted in light of the rich breakfast they'd had at Mikhail's and the lunch they enjoyed with Vincenzo and Angela).

They decided to check the place out. It would be a shame not to try it! If there was a table available, great. If not, they'd just head back. Of course there were no tables: the restaurant was brimming with diners enjoying the magical atmosphere.

As if coming across an oasis after hours of thirsty wandering, Reut and Bernard allowed their curiosity to take precedence over their schedule, and waited patiently for a table to open up. Just as the couple had described, the restaurant was difficult to track down. It was located up on a hill and required quite a bit of hiking to reach it (Vincenzo's tote bags along with twisting staircases made for a rather challenging combination). The restaurant was hidden from the street, emanating intoxicating aromas and offering a beautiful vista as promised. Reut immediately thought about Jean-Claude, how happy he would have been to be there with her. Guiltily, she acknowledged that she was glad he wasn't there.

Something happened between her and Bernard over dinner. Reut couldn't say what it was exactly. On the surface of it, nothing had changed. The conversation remained mostly comfortable and effortless, as it had been throughout the day. They laughed a lot, cutting each other off, talking about everything and nothing. But unlike their talk throughout the day, now the words were no longer just words, the stories no longer just stories. Something had been added to them, expressed through them. Something elusive: a certain depth, an intuitive understanding of one another. Intimacy.

And along with the intimacy came secrets. Other people's secrets, mostly. Bernard shared many details about the Grigoryevs with Reut that he should have kept to himself. Since he was one of the few people who knew these details, if Reut spilled even the tiniest bean and the information started making the rounds, perhaps leaking to the media, Bernard would have been in an uncomfortable position with the writer. But in Bernard's defense, she hardly felt like he was telling her anything she didn't already know. Most of it was obvious, if not official. All she needed was confirmation.

Katya and Pavel had been together, years ago. It wasn't a serious relationship. A month at most. And yet, it was a meaningful month for both of them, verifying that they were meant to be best friends and nothing more. They'd known each other since elementary school, had attended the same high school, were part of the same circle of friends at university. Always symbiotic, communicating in their own way, touching each other affectionately, even kissing hello on the lips. When they finally had their month of romance during college, Mikhail was still just Pavel's younger, introverted brother. An odd brother who barely spoke. He spent most of his days reading or writing, and sharing neither of these passions with others. He admired Pavel and feared him, emotions that did not change much over the years, perhaps only softening a bit as Mikhail moved to Paris and enjoyed meteoric success as a writer.

But there was more. Reut sensed something hiding behind Bernard's "that's all I know" and "this is just my opinion." Something was bothering him as he described these characters. Bernard made a valiant effort to stop himself from divulging as much as he later did, but the words left his mouth almost by accident. Pavel, she learned from Bernard, had been depressed for years, and had a long history of suicide attempts. He had also been broke for years, or at least he said he was, which didn't stop him from living lavishly on his brother's dime. Grigoryev wanted to help him get his life back on track. He worried about him.

"But believe me," Bernard protested, "there's no reason to worry about Pavel. If anything, we should worry about *Mikhail*. He's completely blind to Pavel's manipulations. He does everything the man asks him to. Ugh! And you can't say anything about it! It is completely forbidden to say a bad word about Pavel."

Bernard picked up his glass, all aflame. He began to take a sip, then thought better of it and returned the glass to the table. "And the truly unbearable thing is that, no matter how well Mikhail does, Pavel always finds ways to belittle him. To manipulate him. And Mikhail either doesn't see it or doesn't care. Big brother complex, but what do I know..."

A tense silence. A fine time to take another sip of wine.

"Forget what I said! It's—I said nothing."

Reut didn't give it another thought until they got on the train. She didn't have any time to think before that. It was time to digest the night's memories, and etch them into her mind so that they might later resurface, saddening and exciting her. Then they walked onto the platform, and something in their dynamic transformed almost instantly. Or perhaps it was something in their individual moods, each wishing for a moment's peace.

The train left the station, and it seemed as if the weight of their shared experiences—all those conversations, sights, people, foods, the Ostuni steps—suddenly struck and stilled them. Bernard closed his eyes right away, trying to fall asleep. Reut couldn't follow suit. Her body was tired, but her head was churning. It was time to piece together the day's events, to intertwine them into a neat narrative. Perhaps putting things in order would help her figure out what had transpired.

Because she just didn't understand. Nothing about it made sense. That sadness that struck all of a sudden, that distress that swelled within her as she recounted the magical day. Why? And why the hell was she feeling that pain down there again? Things had improved after her long morning shower, and the pain had vanished almost completely in Ostuni. She thought it was over, that it was behind her.

An acute burning sensation, a tingling in her crotch, a need to touch it, she had to touch it, to press down on her underwear, to tame the pain. But she couldn't.

She needed to touch it! Why did it hurt so much?

She couldn't.

Deep breath.

No, she couldn't. She couldn't! Like a mantra, the words kept echoing, amplifying her fright and her pain. She glanced at Bernard. His eyes were closed. Good. She fixed her gaze on the seatback in front of her, trying to soothe herself. Still the mantra played softly through her mind: she couldn't do it.

What to do?

Nothing to do. And the pain! She couldn't handle it.

She got up.

She felt a need to cry out, but her mouth remained pursed, her forehead furrowed and her eyes squinted.

She got up. The bathroom, she had to find it. But where was it? Everything was difficult. Her entire being gave itself over to this painful attack, to overwhelming terror. She knew she was overreacting, yes, she was losing control. She had to get a hold of herself. She was in a public place. All she had to do was get to the bathroom and splash a little water on her crotch. Yes, she'd settle down after that.

The bathroom was straight ahead. Excellent.

She opened the door. "Oh God!" she shouted, slamming the door with horror, rubbing her hands on her skirt.

Terribly filthy. Why in God's name would anyone do that? And then not even *flush*? Now she'd never get that image out of her head. And the smell. God, the horrid stench. Why was this happening to her? She couldn't do it. She headed to the next train car. A brisk walk. People spoke to her as she walked by, or at least she thought they did. They asked how she was doing. *Signora, signora*, followed by some other words. She didn't understand what they were saying. She felt hot.

She opened the door of the next bathroom with reserved hope. Maybe?

No! Absolutely not. Too much urine on the floor and on the toilet seat.

Another train car, another attempt. The next bathroom *had* to be bearable. It burned. She passed people swiftly, leaning on empty seats as she went, needing to support herself on something. She walked briskly, almost running. She hated people watching her. Fantastic—Reut, the special attraction! But why were they staring? Oh, she didn't want to know what she looked like.

Three people stood outside of the next bathroom: two small women and an older man, all stunningly Italian-looking. She stood beside them, crossing her arms, eyes on the floor. Why did there have to be so many people?! She didn't know what to do. She simply had to go in next. She turned to the two ladies. They were startled: no decorum, no hello or excuse me. Reut just went ahead and asked if she could cut ahead of them. She wasn't feeling well, she explained in French, then in English, making sure to dramatize her suffering. The women did not understand what she said, but knew right away what she wanted. They clung to her almost relentlessly, patting and rubbing her body, trying to hold her limp hand. The older man came over as well, speaking to her. Everyone waited together with her for the door to finally open.

An attractive woman walked out of the stall. "*Mi scusi*," she said, a diva-like Sicilian smile lighting up her face.

Reut walked inside.

She caught a glimpse of herself in the mirror.

She started to cry.

A muted, restrained cry. There were people waiting outside. Her sweat and her tears mixed together. Reut washed her face, but the sweat was everywhere. Her hair, her belly, her back—they were all drenched. Her blouse was sticky. Her underwear. She was still in pain.

She pulled down her skirt and underwear. How she'd have liked to just take them off right now! But she couldn't do that here. It was crowded and uncomfortable. She bent her knees. She gathered water in her hands, splashing her crotch over and over again. There was no doubt about it: there was something there. Bumps. Yes, she could feel them. Everything was swollen. She bent her head, trying to see. She couldn't reach. There was nothing to see anyway. She knew it already: it was either a urinary tract infection or a yeast infection. It must have been.

The tears returned. This time they were accompanied by loud gasps. She couldn't catch her breath. She placed a hand against her chest, trying to calm herself down. She failed.

Faster, harder gasps. Her belly trembled from the crying.

Sobs of release, of panic. She gave into it, surrendering to its rhythm.

In a single moment, everything became too much: Bernard, Jean-Claude, the infection, Aliza, Sanderson, the PhD—and then going back to Polignano a Mare, back to Paris. Life. Everything was too much for her.

She couldn't do it. She couldn't keep it all in anymore.

But what was going on with her? Too many things she didn't understand. First of all, this UTI—where did it come from? How was it even possible? Reut hadn't had this problem for years! Infections belonged to different times, the days before Jean-Claude. They typically appeared at the start of new relationships or toward their end. When her heart grew suspicious, so did her genitals.

But now? No, it didn't make any sense. Her heart, her body, they knew Jean-Claude so well! His sexual satisfaction made her life easier, in a way: Jean-Claude's pleasure was enough for them both.

Then why was she crying for Bernard, too?

Where did this sudden need come from, to have him desire her? Touch her? Odder still, why did she have this fantastical idea that he might want the same thing?

She wasn't all right.

She would say goodbye to Bernard. They would be back in Polignano a Mare soon, and everything would be just like before. Marion. Jean-Claude. The day was over.

Final silent tears streamed down her face. She dried them and fixed herself up before leaving the bathroom, hoping that no one was waiting outside the door to see her in this state. She couldn't think about it any longer, she had to leave.

The train. It would be pulling into the station soon!

Or had it already?

She opened the door.

The two ladies were still waiting outside the stall, rushing to comfort her. But all she wanted was to know was if she'd missed the Polignano a Mare stop. She tried to ask them, but they didn't respond. They said more and more things in Italian, trying over and over to take her hand, to caress it. But Reut had no time for that. She had to wriggle away from them, to find Bernard. She ran out of the train car, leaving the two stunned women behind.

He was standing in the aisle, leaning over his bag. Reut called his name from a distance, huffing. The relief she felt when she found him was diluted by her fear of his response. He turned toward her, wearing a severe expression. The very same one he had when he was looking for her in Ostuni. He asked where she'd been. He'd been worried.

"Our stop is next," he said. "Hurry up, get ready."

She was alone. Stopping one person after another on the street, asking where she could find a pharmacy still open at this hour. Half of them didn't understand her. The other half, mostly tourists, had no patience to help. Earlier, when she'd asked Bernard to return to Grigoryev's house without her, she told him she needed to go to the pharmacy and buy something that couldn't wait. He insisted on accompanying her but ultimately gave in to her persistent refusal.

She was alone, without heavy bags, without thoughts of Jean-Claude, of Bernard, of Marion, of Paris. She walked among the people, so many people, even at this hour. They held hands, couples indulging in an aimless stroll, in empty words exchanged. They would remember almost none of them, but would commit the atmosphere to memory.

She was alone. This man didn't know where the nearest pharmacy was. Neither did that group of people. She tried again. It still burned. She was full of adrenaline; she couldn't stop her search now. She went on, clambering up a small alleyway, then another. He didn't know either. Neither did they. She kept walking upward. Polignano a Mare, like

Ostuni, had many tiers. A gorgeous bridge came into view. Examining the support beams, she was almost sure it was a relic from Roman times. She continued winding her way up the alleys toward the bridge, pulled along with the swarm of tourists.

Ponte Borbonico di Lama Monachile. She was told that was the name of the bridge. It was rather long and full of traffic. Its railings were adorned with small, bright lamps, like fireflies marking the way, pouring warm light over the faded columns. Reut paused on one side, crowding together with other onlookers taking in the view. She'd seen it from a distance the previous night—the savage Ponte Borbonico di Lama Monachile bay. But close up it looked completely different, both glamorous and formidable.

When she saw it from Giuseppe's trattoria, it had been swallowed up against the backdrop, just another jewel in the multicolored mosaic her eyes had taken in. Now it was the star of the show, demanding that the audience give it their full attention. The people in the front row were lucky enough to get a close look at the scene: the tiny houses weighing down the boulders, fighting for their place; the massive rock formations flanking the turquoise water from both sides, almost meeting in the middle, making the Adriatic Sea resemble a slender bottle of wine.

Reut stayed there for a while, as still as the boulders themselves, while the water and the people around her were in constant movement, endlessly transforming yet appearing the same. Then she pulled away from the railing too, turning into another one of those changing beings momentarily attracted to the gorgeous sight, then going on their way. She walked slowly, for a few minutes just an aimless person crossing the bridge, until she remembered the burning she'd forgotten. With this renewed awareness, the pain returned at once, and she resumed her search for a pharmacy. Someone had to know! This burning couldn't go on!

"Excuse me, *mi scusi, mi scusi*," she repeated, pushing her way toward the bar. "*Mi scusi, mi scusi!*"

"*Ciao!*" the bartender greeted her, vigorously shaking a cocktail.

"*Ciao, mi scusi*, maybe you kno—"

"Sorry," he said with an amused smile. "No English."

"*Mi scusi . . . mi scusi!*" she tried to address the other bartender, failing to grab his attention.

So many people. So much noise. People breathed down her neck, shoving and jostling, as if they were all crowded on the deck of a bobbing ship, moving in tandem with the waves. She placed one hand on the bar. She was dizzy. She closed her eyes, hearing the racket more sharply—the lilting Italian, the joyous squeals of young revelers. *Signora, signora*, she heard. *Signora!*

A glass was placed on the bar.

"*Signora*," the bartender repeated. "Take it."

"What?!"

"For you."

The bartender took Reut's hand and guided it over to the

glass he'd given her. He smiled at her and raised a shot glass, signaling to her to drink with him.

Uncomfortable, she took a stingy sip.

"Come on!" the bartender urged her. He raised his fist and punched the air, feigning a boxing match.

"Where are you from?" asked a young man beside her.

"From Israel," she replied, sipping again. "I mean, from Paris."

The young man was waiting for some drinks alongside a woman with flowing curls. The way he wrapped his arm around the woman's body left no room for doubt—she was either his girlfriend or his escapade for the night. Whatever the case, the two seemed happy to be out together and have a chance to practice their English on Reut. The young man ordered her another drink, urging her to finish the first. He was tall and skinny, his southern tan a wonderful contrast to his green eyes. His partner was a true beauty. Apart from her nose and small cheekbones, everything about her was big and sensual: her eyes, her lips, her breasts, her hair.

Reut accompanied them to another bar. After the third drink, she stopped reminding herself she was talking to kids who were Julian's age. The couple was joined by their friends, the group growing. Everybody took an interest in Reut, so warm and lively; younger versions of Vincenzo and Angela whose entire lives were ahead of them.

She was given another shot. She lost track of how much she was drinking. They were at Piazza Vittorio Emanuele. She laughed at some joke and the conversation around her went on. She took a seat on one of the steps near the church, continuing to pour a cocktail down her throat. She placed the glass on the ground, threw her head back, closed her eyes, and reveled in the dizziness that traveled through her body. Then she got up and kept on walking, faltering drunkenly through the alleys. Her cellphone rang. She rummaged through her bag for it, missing the call. She noticed that her phone's battery was almost dead and a burst of laughter escaped her. Everything was funny all of a sudden, even this. She was thirsty. She walked into another bar, pushing her way through people. She accidentally stepped on someone's foot and burst out laughing again. A man asked her what was so funny, and the question only reignited her laughter.

She waited for him inside the clump of people while he went off looking for some water for her. She downed it in one gulp and they started to talk, raising their voices. The upbeat music took over. Words were meaningless, body language prevailed. He moved closer, repeating himself. His mouth was against her ear. He told her things and all she could feel was the heat emanating from his mouth, his hand holding her arm.

She was hungry. He said all the good trattorias were closed at this hour. All that was left were tourist traps. They went off on a search, wandering happily. She stumbled over a bump in the road and almost fell. It happened again in the next alley, but this time she wasn't so lucky. He offered her his hand and helped her up. Everything's fine, she's fine, really! He rubbed her arm, fixed his eyes on hers.

"*Bella*," he whispered. "So beautiful."

She looked at him too. His face almost surprised her. She was noticing it for the first time. Something about it was repulsive. That messy, tangled beard. She didn't like it. It didn't go with his carefully manicured mustache. His eyes were too close together and made her uncomfortable: he was ogling her with so much lust and excessive confidence that it seemed unnatural.

"I'm hungry," she said.

The search went on.

Fresh cocktail in hand. She couldn't remember when he gave it to her, but she gulped it down with gusto. They were waiting in line at a pizzeria. His hand on her back, moving up and down, rubbing. Finally, his name was called. She moved away from the line while he paid, swept up in a wave of scattered thoughts about her day with Bernard. He returned with the hot tray, lightly cupping her buttocks to pull her out of her reveries.

She devoured the first two slices, took a third one, asked him why he wasn't eating. He shoved his tongue into her mouth. It came out of nowhere. Her body was warm. It felt good. She was pulled into him—lips, teeth, tongue. Everything was sucked into that powerful tornado that had become faceless again. He fondled her body, pressed her hand against his genitals. "Feel it," he whispered, "see what you're doing to it." She wiped the spit off her chin. She needed to use the bathroom.

"We'll find you a bathroom in a minute," he said, pulling her to her feet. "Good girl . . ."

ANOTHER MORNING

Reut woke from a deep sleep a little after ten in the morning. She had no memory of when or how she'd fallen asleep. She stood up quickly, growing dizzy. She spent a few minutes massaging her temples, feeling her stomach churn, then sat back down and buried her head in her hands. Total darkness. Then red and blue flashes started to appear against the black backdrop, the light in the room bursting through the dimness, reminding her where she was. She turned her head back and watched him for a few seconds. He was still asleep, lying in his usual position, flat as a plank.

"God," she muttered, shoving her head into her hands again.

The events of the previous night came flooding back, without any recollection of how she'd made her way back to the house, who had helped her get there, and who had been there to greet her. What had happened last night?

Something had taken over her.

She pulled herself up from bed slowly and walked to the bathroom. The burning sensation had returned, but she didn't want to think about that, or anything else. She wasn't about to let this day be a direct continuation of yesterday. But the distress refused to let up: heaviness with every footstep, a constant pressure in her chest, as if she were in mourning.

She walked into the bathroom, locked herself inside, and paused, leaning against the door. Then she slowly peeled off her robe and laid it out on the counter. She was awfully nauseous. She leaned over the sink, shoved a finger down her throat, hoping that vomit would wash out the alcohol. She coughed, her eyes welling up. She tried again, this time pushing the finger deeper, as if there was a secret reservoir of vomit she was seeking to tap. A little liquid came out. She tried again, unsuccessfully. Her body refused to let everything out.

She removed her underwear, standing still in front of the mirror for a few moments. Her eyes looked straight ahead, seeing nothing. She reached her hand down and gently patted her crotch. Everything was still swollen. She walked into the shower, turned on the faucet, waited a few moments until the temperature was satisfactory. The water found her face, warming it. She closed her eyes, letting her neck fall back. A few minutes, then all of a sudden a stream of urine released. It burned! The train had returned, she experienced it anew— flashes of herself running between bathrooms, searching, panting, unable to contain her panic. Then, inside the stall, collapsing, watching herself fall apart. Then the Italian slipping his tongue inside her, touching her, feeling her up, pleasing her. She couldn't remember what he looked like.

She wanted to weep, just like yesterday. She saw herself inside the train toilet, miserable, absurd, and all she wanted to do was cry. What had come over her? Had she already used up her tears? She stared at the glass pane of the shower. The tears weren't going to come this morning. She settled herself on the floor, leaning back against the wall, folding her knees against her breasts, and let her mouth hang slackly open as the water flowed over her face and across her lips and slipped down into the drain.

DANA SHEM-UR lived in Paris for three years and obtained a master's degree in philosophy from the École Normale Supérieure. She is a Ph.D. candidate in history at Tel Aviv University who translates from French, Italian, and Chinese into Hebrew.

YARDENNE GREENSPAN has translated writing by Israeli authors including Shemi Zarhin, Yitzhak Gormezano-Goren, Shimon Adaf, Yishai Sarid, and Alex Epstein.

DISTANT FATHERS
BY MARINA JARRE

This singular autobiography unfurls from the author's native Latvia during the 1920s and '30s and expands southward to the Italian countryside. In distinctive writing as poetic as it is precise, Marina Jarre depicts an exceptionally multinational and complicated family. This memoir probes questions of time, language, womanhood, belonging and estrangement, while asking what homeland can be for those who have none, or many more than one.

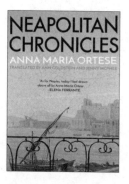

NEAPOLITAN CHRONICLES
BY ANNA MARIA ORTESE

A classic of European literature, this superb collection of fiction and reportage is set in Italy's most vibrant and turbulent metropolis—Naples—in the immediate aftermath of World War Two. These writings helped inspire Elena Ferrante's best-selling novels and she has expressed deep admiration for Ortese.

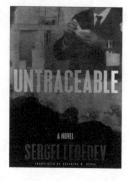

UNTRACEABLE
BY SERGEI LEBEDEV

An extraordinary Russian novel about poisons of all kinds: physical, moral and political. Professor Kalitin is a ruthless, narcissistic chemist who has developed an untraceable lethal poison called Neophyte while working in a secret city on an island in the Russian far east. When the Soviet Union collapses, he defects to the West in a riveting tale through which Lebedev probes the ethical responsibilities of scientists providing modern tyrants with ever newer instruments of retribution and control.

And the Bride Closed the Door
by Ronit Matalon

A young bride shuts herself up in a bedroom on her wedding day, refusing to get married. In this moving and humorous look at contemporary Israel and the chaotic ups and downs of love everywhere, her family gathers outside the locked door, not knowing what to do. The only communication they receive from behind the door are scribbled notes, one of them a cryptic poem about a prodigal daughter returning home. The harder they try to reach the defiant woman, the more the despairing groom is convinced that her refusal should be respected. But what, exactly, ought to be respected? Is this merely a case of cold feet?

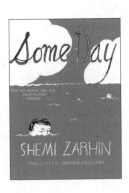

Some Day
by Shemi Zarhin

On the shores of Israel's Sea of Galilee lies the city of Tiberias, a place bursting with sexuality and longing for love. The air is saturated with smells of cooking and passion. *Some Day* is a gripping family saga, a sensual and emotional feast that plays out over decades. This is an enchanting tale about tragic fates that disrupt families and break our hearts. Zarhin's hypnotic writing renders a painfully delicious vision of individual lives behind Israel's larger national story.

Alexandrian Summer
by Yitzhak Gormezano Goren

This is the story of two Jewish families living their frenzied last days in the doomed cosmopolitan social whirl of Alexandria just before fleeing Egypt for Israel in 1951. The conventions of the Egyptian upper-middle class are laid bare in this dazzling novel, which exposes sexual hypocrisies and portrays a vanished polyglot world of horse racing, seaside promenades and nightclubs.

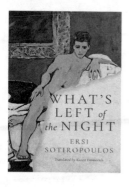

What's Left of the Night
by Ersi Sotiropoulos

Constantine Cavafy arrives in Paris in 1897 on a trip that will deeply shape his future and push him toward his poetic inclination. With this lyrical novel, tinged with an hallucinatory eroticism that unfolds over three unforgettable days, celebrated Greek author Ersi Sotiropoulos depicts Cavafy in the midst of a journey of self-discovery across a continent on the brink of massive change. A stunning portrait of a budding author—before he became C.P. Cavafy, one of the 20th century's greatest poets—that illuminates the complex relationship of art, life, and the erotic desires that trigger creativity.

The 6:41 to Paris
by Jean-Philippe Blondel

Cécile, a stylish 47-year-old, has spent the weekend visiting her parents outside Paris. By Monday morning, she's exhausted. These trips back home are stressful and she settles into a train compartment with an empty seat beside her. But it's soon occupied by a man she recognizes as Philippe Leduc, with whom she had a passionate affair that ended in her brutal humiliation 30 years ago. In the fraught hour and a half that ensues, Cécile and Philippe hurtle towards the French capital in a psychological thriller about the pain and promise of past romance.

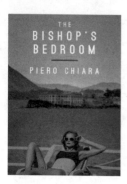

The Bishop's Bedroom
by Piero Chiara

World War Two has just come to an end and there's a yearning for renewal. A man in his thirties is sailing on Lake Maggiore in northern Italy, hoping to put off the inevitable return to work. Dropping anchor in a small, fashionable port, he meets the enigmatic owner of a nearby villa. The two form an uneasy bond, recognizing in each other a shared taste for idling and erotic adventure. A sultry, stylish psychological thriller executed with supreme literary finesse.

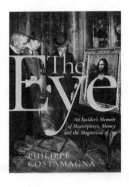

THE EYE
BY PHILIPPE COSTAMAGNA

It's a rare and secret profession, comprising a few dozen people around the world equipped with a mysterious mixture of knowledge and innate sensibility. Summoned to Swiss bank vaults, Fifth Avenue apartments, and Tokyo storerooms, they are entrusted by collectors, dealers, and museums to decide if a coveted picture is real or fake and to determine if it was painted by Leonardo da Vinci or Raphael. *The Eye* lifts the veil on the rarified world of connoisseurs devoted to the authentication and discovery of Old Master artworks.

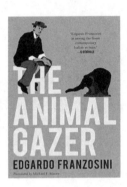

THE ANIMAL GAZER
BY EDGARDO FRANZOSINI

A hypnotic novel inspired by the strange and fascinating life of sculptor Rembrandt Bugatti, brother of the fabled automaker. Bugatti obsessively observes and sculpts the baboons, giraffes, and panthers in European zoos, finding empathy with their plight and identifying with their life in captivity. Rembrandt Bugatti's work, now being rediscovered, is displayed in major art museums around the world and routinely fetches large sums at auction. Edgardo Franzosini recreates the young artist's life with intense lyricism, passion, and sensitivity.

ALLMEN AND THE DRAGONFLIES
BY MARTIN SUTER

Johann Friedrich von Allmen has exhausted his family fortune by living in Old World grandeur despite present-day financial constraints. Forced to downscale, Allmen inhabits the garden house of his former Zurich estate, attended by his Guatemalan butler, Carlos. This is the first of a series of humorous, fast-paced detective novels devoted to a memorable gentleman thief. A thrilling art heist escapade infused with European high culture and luxury that doesn't shy away from the darker side of human nature.

The Madeleine Project
by Clara Beaudoux

A young woman moves into a Paris apartment and discovers a storage room filled with the belongings of the previous owner, a certain Madeleine who died in her late nineties, and whose treasured possessions nobody seems to want. In an audacious act of journalism driven by personal curiosity and humane tenderness, Clara Beaudoux embarks on *The Madeleine Project*, documenting what she finds on Twitter with text and photographs, introducing the world to an unsung 20th century figure.

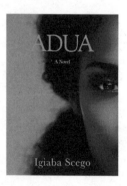

Adua
by Igiaba Scego

Adua, an immigrant from Somalia to Italy, has lived in Rome for nearly forty years. She came seeking freedom from a strict father and an oppressive regime, but her dreams of film stardom ended in shame. Now that the civil war in Somalia is over, her homeland calls her. She must decide whether to return and reclaim her inheritance, but also how to take charge of her own story and build a future.

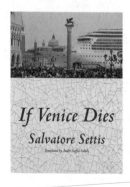

If Venice Dies
by Salvatore Settis

Internationally renowned art historian Salvatore Settis ignites a new debate about the Pearl of the Adriatic and cultural patrimony at large. In this fiery blend of history and cultural analysis, Settis argues that "hit-and-run" visitors are turning Venice and other landmark urban settings into shopping malls and theme parks. This is a passionate plea to secure the soul of Venice, written with consummate authority, wide-ranging erudition and élan.

The Madonna of Notre Dame
by Alexis Ragougneau

Fifty thousand people jam into Notre Dame Cathedral to celebrate the Feast of the Assumption. The next morning, a beautiful young woman clothed in white kneels at prayer in a cathedral side chapel. But when someone accidentally bumps against her, her body collapses. She has been murdered. This thrilling novel illuminates shadowy corners of the world's most famous cathedral, shedding light on good and evil with suspense, compassion and wry humor.

The Last Weynfeldt
by Martin Suter

Adrian Weynfeldt is an art expert in an international auction house, a bachelor in his mid-fifties living in a grand Zurich apartment filled with costly paintings and antiques. Always correct and well-mannered, he's given up on love until one night—entirely out of character for him—Weynfeldt decides to take home a ravishing but unaccountable young woman and gets embroiled in an art forgery scheme that threatens his buttoned up existence. This refined page-turner moves behind elegant bourgeois facades into darker recesses of the heart.

Moving the Palace
by Charif Majdalani

A young Lebanese adventurer explores the wilds of Africa, encountering an eccentric English colonel in Sudan and enlisting in his service. In this lush chronicle of far-flung adventure, the military recruit crosses paths with a compatriot who has dismantled a sumptuous palace and is transporting it across the continent on a camel caravan. This is a captivating modern-day Odyssey in the tradition of Bruce Chatwin and Paul Theroux.

New Vessel Press

To purchase these titles and for more information please visit newvesselpress.com.